Peeps at Many Lands:
Egypt

R. Talbot Kelly

Contents

PEEPS AT MANY LANDS:
EGYPT

BY

R. Talbot Kelly

CHAPTER 1
ITS ANTIQUITY

Every boy or girl who has read the history of Joseph must often have wondered what kind of a country Egypt might be, and tried to picture to themselves the scenes so vividly suggested in the Bible story.

It must have been a startling experience for the little shepherd boy, who, stolen from his home among the quiet hills of Canaan, so suddenly found himself an inmate of a palace, and, in his small way, a participator in the busy whirl of life of a royal city.

No contrast could possibly have been greater than between his simple pastoral life spent in tending the flocks upon the hillsides and the magnificence of the city of Pharaoh, and how strange a romance it is to think of the little slave boy eventually becoming the virtual ruler of the most wealthy and most highly cultured country in the world!

And then in course of time the very brothers who had so cruelly sold him into bondage were forced by famine to come to Joseph as suppliants for food, and, in their descendants, presently to become the meanest slaves in the land, persecuted and oppressed until their final deliverance by Moses.

How long ago it all seems when we read these old Bible stories! Yet, when 4,000 years ago necessity compelled Abraham, with Sarah his wife, to stay awhile in Egypt, they were lodged at Tanis, a royal city founded by one of a succession of kings which for 3,000 years before Abraham's day had governed the land, and modern discoveries have proved that even before *that* time there were other kings and an earlier civilization.

How interesting it is to know that to-day we may still find records of these early Bible times in the sculptured monuments which are scattered all over the land, and to know that in the hieroglyphic writings which adorn the walls of tombs or temples many of the events we there read about are narrated.

Many of the temples were built by the labour of the oppressed Israelites, others were standing long before Moses confounded their priests or besought Pharaoh to liberate his people. We may ourselves stand in courts where, perhaps, Joseph took part in some temple rite, while the huge canal called the "Bahr Yusef" (or river of Joseph), which he built 6,300 years ago, still supplies the province Fayoum with water.

Ancient Tanis also, from whose tower Abraham saw "wonders in the field of Zoan," still exists in a heap of ruins, extensive enough to show how great a city it had been, and from its mounds the writer has often witnessed the strange mirage which excited the wonder of the patriarch.

Everywhere throughout the land are traces of the children of Israel, many of whose descendants still remain in the land of Goshen, and in every instance where fresh discovery has thrown light upon the subject the independent record of history found in hieroglyph or papyrus confirms the Bible narrative, so that we may be quite sure when we read these old stories that they are not merely legends, open to doubt, but are the true histories of people who actually lived.

As you will see from what I have told you, Egypt is perhaps the oldest country in the world--the oldest, that is, in civilization. No one quite knows how old it is, and no record has been discovered to tell us.

All through the many thousands of years of its history Egypt has had a great influence upon other nations, and although the ancient Persians, Greeks, and Romans successively dominated it, these conquering races have each in turn disappeared, while Egypt goes on as ever, and its people remain.

Egypt has been described as the centre of the world, and if we look at the map we will see how true this is. Situated midway between Europe, Africa, and Asia in the old days of land caravans, most of the trade between these continents passed through her hands, while her ports on the Mediterranean controlled the sea trade of the Levant.

All this helped to make Egypt wealthy, and gave it great political importance, so that very early in the world's history it enjoyed a greater prosperity and a higher civilization than any of its neighbours. Learned men from all countries were drawn to it in search of fresh knowledge, for nowhere else were there such seats of learning as in the Nile cities, and it is acknowledged that the highly trained priesthood of the Pharaohs practised arts and sciences of which we in these days are ignorant, and have failed to discover.

In 30 B.C. the last of the Pharaohs disappeared, and for 400 years the Romans ruled in Egypt, many of their emperors restoring the ancient temples as well as building new ones; but all the Roman remains in Egypt are poor in comparison with the real Egyptian art, and, excepting for a few small temples, little now remains of their buildings but the heaps of rubbish which surround the magnificent monuments of Egypt's great period.

During the Roman occupation Christianity became the recognized religion of the country, and to-day the Copts (who are the real descendants of the ancient Egyptians) still preserve the primitive faith of those early times, and, with the Abyssinians, are perhaps the oldest Christian church now existing.

The greatest change in the history of Egypt, however, and the one that has left the most permanent effect upon it, was the Mohammedan invasion in A.D. 640, and I must tell you something about this, because to the great majority of people who visit Egypt the two great points of interest are its historical remains and the beautiful art of the Mohammedans. The times of the Pharaohs are in the past, and have the added interest of association with the Bible; this period of antiquity is a special study for the historian and the few who are able to decipher hieroglyphic writing, but the Mohammedan era, though commencing nearly 200 years before Egbert was crowned first King of England, continues to the present day, and the beautiful mosques, as their churches are called (many of which were built long before there were any churches in our own country), are still used by the Moslems.

Nothing in history is so remarkable as the sudden rise to power of the followers of Mohammed. An ill-taught, half-savage people, coming from an unknown part of Arabia, in a very few years they had become masters of Syria, Asia Minor, Persia, and Egypt, and presently extended their religion all through North Africa, and even conquered the southern half of Spain, and to-day the Faith of Islam, as their religion is called, is the third largest in the world.

Equally surprising as their accession to power is the very beautiful art they created, first in Egypt and then throughout Tunis, Algeria, Morocco, and Spain.

The Moslem churches in Cairo are extremely beautiful, and of a style quite unlike anything that the world had known before. Some of my readers, perhaps, may have seen pictures of them and of the Alhambra in Spain, probably the most elegant and ornate palace ever built.

No country in the world gives one so great a sense of age as Egypt, and although it has many beauties, and the life of the people to-day is most picturesque, as we will presently see, it is its extreme antiquity which most excites the imagination, for, while the whole Bible history from Abraham to the Apostles covers a period of only 2,000 years, the known history of Egypt commenced as far back as 6,000 years ago! From the sphinx at Ghizeh, which is so ancient that no one knows its origin, to the great dam at Assuan, monument of its present day, each period of its history has left *some* record, some tomb or temple, which we may study, and it is this more than anything else which makes Egypt so attractive to thoughtful people.

CHAPTER II
THE LAND

It would naturally be supposed that a country which for so long a time exercised such influence upon the world at large would be extensive and densely populated.

Neither is the case, however, for though upon the map Egypt appears to be a large country, the greater part consists of rock and burning sand, and is practically uninhabited.

The *real* land of Egypt is the narrow strip of alluvial soil which forms the Nile banks, and the fertile delta which spreads fan-like from Cairo to the sea. These two divisions of the land practically constitute Upper and Lower Egypt. In area each is less than Wales, while the total population of the country is not twice that of London.

It is its extreme fertility which has made Egypt prosperous, and throughout the world's history it has been a granary for the nations, for while drought and famine might affect other lands, Egypt has always been able to supply food to its neighbours.

How does this come about? Let me try and explain.

Thousands of years ago, when the world was very young, the whole land was covered by the sea, which is plainly shown by the fossils embedded in the rocks, and which lie scattered over its highest deserts.

As the sea receded, the Nile, then a mighty river, began to cut its channel through the rock, and poured into the sea somewhere about where Cairo now stands.

As the ages passed the river cut deeper and deeper into its rocky bed, leaving on either side the mountains which hem in its narrow valley, and at the same time depositing along its banks and in the delta forming at its mouth the rich alluvial mud which it had carried with it from the heart of Africa.

In this way the Egypt of history has been formed, but, surrounded as it is by sandy wastes, and often swept by hot desert winds, no rain falls to bring life to the fields, or enable the rich soil to produce the crops which are its source of wealth.

Nature provides a remedy, however, and the river which first formed the land is also its life-giver, for every year the Nile overflows its banks, re-fertilizing the soil, and filling the canals and reservoirs with water sufficient for the year's needs, without which Egypt would remain a barren, sun-baked land, instead of the fertile country it is.

The first view of Egypt as it is approached from the sea is disappointing, for the low-lying delta is hardly raised at all above sea-level, and its monotony is only broken by an occasional hillock or the lofty minarets of the coast towns.

Formerly the Nile had several mouths, and from many seaports Egypt carried on its trade with the outside world. To-day only Rosetta and Damietta remain to give their names to the two branches by which alone the Nile now seeks the sea. These interesting seaports, mediÃ¡val and richly picturesque, are no longer the prosperous cities they once were, for railways have diverted traffic from the Nile, and nearly all the seaborne trade of Egypt is now carried from Alexandria or Port Said, the northern entrance to the Suez Canal, and it is by either of these two ports that modern visitors make their entry into Egypt.

Alexandria is interesting as the city founded by Alexander the Great, but with the exception of Pompey's pillar and its ancient catacombs has little attraction for visitors. The town is almost entirely Italian in character, and is peopled by so many different races that it hardly seems Egypt at all; boys, however, would enjoy a visit to the Ras-el-Tīn Fort, which figured so largely in the bombardment of Alexandria, and away to the east, near Rosetta, is Aboukīr Bay, the scene of a more stirring fight, for it was here that, in A.D. 1798, Nelson destroyed the French fleet,[1] and secured for Britain the command of the Mediterranean.

After the monotony of a sea voyage, landing at Port Said is amusing. The steamer anchors in mid-stream, and is quickly surrounded by gaily painted shore boats, whose swarthy occupants--half native, half Levantine--clamber on board,

---

1   In the "Battle of the Nile."

and clamour and wrangle for the possession of your baggage. They are noisy fellows, but once your boatman is selected, landing at the little stages which lie in the harbour is quickly effected, and you and your belongings are safely deposited at the station, and your journey to Cairo begun.

Port Said is a rambling town, whose half brick, half timber buildings have a general air of dilapidation and unfinish which is depressing. The somewhat picturesque principal bazaar street is soon exhausted, and excepting for the imposing offices of the Suez Canal Company, and the fine statue to De Lesseps, recently erected on the breakwater, Port Said has little else to excite the curiosity of the visitors; built upon a mud-bank formed of Suez Canal dredgings, its existence is its most interesting feature, and the white breakers of the Mediterranean, above which it is so little raised, seem ever ready to engulf it as they toss and tumble upon its narrow beach.

Leaving Port Said behind, the train travels slowly along the canal bank, and we begin to enter Egypt.

On the right the quiet waters of Lake Menzala, fringed with tall reeds and eucalyptus trees, stretches to the far horizon, where quaintly shaped fishing-boats disappear with their cargoes towards distant Damietta. Thousands of wild birds, duck of all kinds, ibis and pelican, fish in the shallows, or with the sea-gulls wheel in dense masses in the air, for this is a reservation as a breeding-green for wild-fowl, where they are seldom, if ever, disturbed.

On the left is the Suez Canal, the world's highway to the Far East, and ships of all nations pass within a stone's throw of your train. Between, and in strange contrast with the blueness of the canal, runs a little watercourse, reed fringed, and turbid in its rapid flow. This is the "sweet-water" canal, and gives its name to one of our engagements with Arabi's army, and which, from the far-distant Nile, brings fresh water to supply Port Said and the many stations on its route.

To the south and east stretches the mournful desert in which the Israelites began their forty years of wandering, and which thousands of Moslems annually traverse on their weary pilgrimage to Mecca; while in all directions is mirage, so perfect in its deception as to mislead the most experienced of travellers at times.

Roaming over the desert which hems in the delta, solitary shepherds, strangely clad and wild-looking, herd their flocks of sheep and goats which browse upon the scrub. These are the descendants of those same Ishmaelites who sold Joseph into Egypt, and the occasional encampment of some Bedouin tribe shows us something of the life which the patriarchs might have led.

In contrast with the desert, the delta appears very green and fertile, for we are quickly in the land of Goshen, most beautiful, perhaps, of all the delta provinces.

The country is very flat and highly cultivated. In all directions, as far as the eye can see, broad stretches of corn wave in the gentle breeze, while brilliant patches of clover or the quieter-coloured onion crops vary the green of the landscape. The scent of flowering bean-fields fills the air, and the hum of wild bees is heard above the other sounds of the fields. Palm groves lift their feathery plumes towards the sky, and mulberry-trees and dark-toned tamarisks shade the water-wheels, which, with incessant groanings, are continually turned by blindfolded bullocks. Villages and little farmsteads are frequent, and everywhere are the people, men, women, and children, working on the land which so richly rewards their labour.

The soil is very rich, and, given an ample water-supply, produces two or three crops a year, while the whole surface is so completely under cultivation that there is no room left for grass or wild flowers to grow. Many crops are raised besides those I have already mentioned, such as maize, barley, rice, and flax, and in the neighbourhood of towns and villages radishes, cucumbers, melons, and tomatoes are plentifully grown. Formerly wheat was Egypt's principal crop, but since its introduction by Mohammed Ali in A.D. 1820, **cotton** has taken first place amongst its products, and is of so fine a quality that it is the dearest in the world, and is used almost entirely for mixing with silk or the manufacture of sateen. Cotton, however, is very exhausting to the soil, and where it is grown the land must have its intervals of rest.

No sooner is one crop gathered than yokes of oxen, drawing strangely shaped wooden ploughs, prepare the land for another; and the newly turned soil looks black against the vivid clover fields, in which tethered cattle graze; while large flocks of sheep of many colours, in which brown predominates, follow the ploughs and feed upon the stubble, for the native is as economical as he is industrious.

Peopled by a race of born farmers, and in soil and climate provided by Nature with all that could be desired for crop-raising, only rain is lacking to bring the fields to fruition, and from the earliest times a great system of irrigation has existed in

Egypt. It is curious to see in many directions the white lateen sails of boats which appear to be sailing over the fields. In reality they are sailing on the canals which intersect the country in all directions, and by means of thousands of water-wheels and pumps supply the land with water. Though the Nile overflows its banks, its inundation does not cover the whole land; so great arterial canals which are filled at high Nile have been constructed throughout the country. From these, smaller canals branch right and left, carrying the water to the furthest corners of the land, while such boundary marks as exist to separate different estates or farms usually take the form of a watercourse.

These canal banks form the highways of the country, and are thronged by travellers and laden camels, while large flocks of sheep and goats are herded along their sloping sides. Every here and there are little enclosures, spread with clean straw or mats, and surrounded by a fence of cornstalks or low walls of mud. These are the holy places where in the intervals of work the devout Moslem may say his prayers; and, often bowered by shady trees, a whitewashed dome marks the burial-place of some saint or village notable.

The scenery of the delta, though flat, is luxuriant; for Mohammed Ali not only introduced cotton into Egypt, but compelled the people to plant trees, so that the landscape is varied by large groves of date-palms, and the sycamores and other trees which surround the villages and give shade to the paths and canal banks. It is a pastoral land, luxuriantly green; and how beautiful it is as the night falls, and the last of the sunset lingers in the dew-laden air, wreathed with the smoke of many fires; and, as the stars one by one appear in the darkening sky, and the labour of the field ceases, the lowing cattle wend their slow ways toward the villages and the bull-frogs in their thousands raise their evensong. No scenery in the world has, to my mind, such mellow and serene beauty as these farm-lands of Lower Egypt, and in a later chapter I will tell you more about them, and of the simple people whose life is spent in the fields.

CHAPTER III
CAIRO--I

Usually its capital may be taken as typical of its country; but in Egypt this is not so. Cairo is essentially different from anything else in Egypt, not only in its buildings and architecture, but in the type and mode of life of its inhabitants.

How shall I give you any real idea of a city which is often considered to be the most beautiful Oriental capital in the world, as it is certainly one of the most interesting? From a distance, looking across the fields of Shoubra,[2] it is very beautiful, especially at sunset, when beyond the dark green foliage of the sycamore and cypress trees which rise above the orange groves, the domes and minarets of the native quarter gleam golden in the sunlight. Behind is the citadel, crowned by Mohammed Ali's tomb-mosque of white marble, whose tall twin minarets seem to tower above the rosy-tinted heights of the Mokattam Hills. Even here the noise of the city reaches you in a subdued hum, for Cairo is not only a large city, but it is densely populated, and contains nearly a twelfth part of the whole population of Egypt. Away towards the sunset the pyramids stand out clearly against the glowing sky, and the tall masts and sails of the Nile boats reach high above the palm groves and buildings which screen the river from view.

Cairo consists of two distinct and widely different parts, the Esbikiyeh and Ismailieh quarters of the west end, built for and almost entirely occupied by Europeans, and the purely native town, whose streets and bazaars, mosques and palaces, have remained practically unchanged for centuries.

At one time the European quarters were in many ways charming, though too much like some fashionable continental town to be altogether picturesque; but of

2 A distant suburb of Cairo.

late years the shady avenues and gardens of the west end have entirely disappeared to make way for streets of commercial buildings, while the new districts of Kasr-el-Dubara and Ghezireh have arisen to house the well-to-do. Our interest in Cairo, therefore, is centred in the native quarters, where miles of streets and alleys, rich in Arabesque buildings, are untouched except by the mellowing hand of Time.

It is difficult at first to form any true idea of native Cairo; its life is so varied and its interests so diverse that the new-comer is bewildered.

Types of many races, clad in strange Eastern costumes, crowd the narrow streets, which are overlooked by many beautiful buildings whose dark shadows lend additional glory to the sunlight. Richly carved doorways give glimpses of cool courts and gardens within the houses, while awnings of many colours shade the bazaars and shopping streets.

Heavily laden camels and quaint native carts with difficulty thread their way through the crowd, amongst which little children, clad in the gayest of dresses, play their games. Goats and sheep pick up a living in the streets, clearing it of garbage, and often feeding more generously, though surreptitiously, from a fruit or vegetable shop. Hawks and pigeons wheel and circle in the air, which is filled with the scent of incense and the sound of the street cries. Everywhere is movement and bustle, and the glowing colour of the buildings and costumes of every tint and texture.

Let us study a little more closely the individual types and occupations that make up the life of the streets, and a pleasant way in which to do so is to seat oneself on the high bench of some native café, where, undisturbed by the traffic, we may watch the passers-by.

The cafés themselves play an important part in the life of the people, being a rendezvous not only for the refreshment provided, but for gossip and the inter-change of news. They are very numerous all over the city, and are generally fronted by three or more wooden archways painted in some bright colour and open to the street. Outside are the "dekkas," or high benches, on which, sitting cross-legged, the customer enjoys his coffee or his pipe. Indoors are a few chairs, and the square tiled platform on which are placed the cooking-pots and little charcoal fire of the café-keeper. Generally an awning of canvas covered with patches of coloured cloth screens you from the sun, or gives shelter from the occasional winter showers which clear the streets of passengers and render them a sea of mud, for the streets are unpaved and no drainage exists to carry off the surface water.

The cafÃ©-owner is always polite, and glad to see you, and the coffee he makes is nearly always excellent, though few of his European guests would care to regale themselves with the curiously shaped water-pipes with which the native intoxicates himself with opium or "hashÏsh," and which are used indiscriminately by all the customers.

Like most of the small tradesmen, our host is clad in a "gelabieh," or long gown of white or blue cotton, gathered round the waist by a girdle of coloured cloth. Stuck jauntily on the back of his head is the red "tarbŪsh," or fez, universal in the towns, or, if married, he wears a turban of fine white cotton; his shoes are of red or yellow leather, but are generally carried in his hand if the streets are muddy.

And now, having noticed our cafÃ© and our host, let us sit comfortably and try and distinguish the various types which go to form the crowd which from dawn to dark throngs the thoroughfares.

First of all it will be noticed how many different trades are carried on in the streets, most prominent of all being that of the water-sellers, for Cairo is hot and dusty, and water is in constant demand.

There are several grades of water-carriers. First, the "sakka," who carries on his back a goat-skin filled with water; one of the fore-legs forms the spout, which is simply held tight in the hand to prevent the water from escaping. He is the poorest of them all, barefooted and wearing an often ragged blue gelabieh, while a leather apron protects his back from the dripping goat-skin. He it is who waters the streets and fills the "zÏrs," or filters, in the shops, a number of shop-keepers combining to employ him to render this service to their section of a street.

A superior grade is the "khamali," who carries upon his back a large earthen pot of filtered water. When he wishes to fill the brass drinking-cups, which he cleverly tinkles as he walks, he has simply to bend forward until the water runs out of the spout above his shoulder and is caught in one of the cups, and it is interesting to notice that he seldom spills a drop.

Then there is that swaggering and often handsome fellow clad in red, and with a coloured scarf around his head, who, with shoulders well set back, carries, slung in a broad leather belt, a terra-cotta jar. This is the "sussi," who sells liquorice water, or a beverage made from prunes, and which he hands to his customers in a dainty blue and white china bowl.

The highest grade of all is the "sherbutli," also gaily dressed, who from an enormous green glass bottle, brass mounted, and cooled by a large lump of ice held in a cradle at the neck, dispenses sherbet, lemonade, or other cooling drink. Each of these classes of water-seller is well patronized, for Egypt is a thirsty land.

Here comes a bread-seller, whose fancy loaves and cakes are made in rings and strung upon wands which project from the rim of a basket; or on a tray of wicker-work or queer little donkey-cart are piled the flat unleavened loaves of the people.

To remind us of the chief baker's dream, the pastry-cook still cries his wares, which, carried in baskets on his head, are often raided by the thieving hawk or crow, while delicious fruits and fresh vegetables are vended from barrows, much like the coster trade in London.

Many of the passers-by are well to do, shop-keepers and merchants, clothed in flowing "khaftan" of coloured cloth or silk, over which, hanging loosely from their shoulders, is the black goat's wool "arbiyeh," or cloak.

The shops also make a gay addition to the general colour scheme. Of these the fruit shop is perhaps the prettiest; here rosy apples and juicy oranges, or pink-fleshed water-melons, are tastefully arranged in baskets or on shelves covered with papers of different tints. Even the tallow-chandler renders his shop attractive by means of festoons of candles, some of enormous size, and all tinted in patterns, while the more important shopping streets are one continuous display of many coloured silks and cotton goods, the glittering wares of the jeweller or coppersmith, and the gay trappings of the saddler.

In between the shops may often be noticed small doorways, whose white plaster is decorated by some bright though crude design in many colours; this is the "hammam," or public bath, while the shop of the barber, chief gossip and story-teller of his quarter, is easily distinguished by the fine-meshed net hung across the entrance as a protection against flies, for flies abound in Cairo, which, however disagreeable they may be, is perhaps fortunate in a country where the laws of sanitation are so lightly regarded.

Noise enters largely into street life, and the native is invariably loud voiced. No bargain is concluded without an apparent squabble, and every tradesman in the street calls his wares, while drivers of vehicles are incessant in their cries of warning to foot-passengers. All the sounds are not unmusical, however, for from the minarets comes the "muezzin's" sweet call to prayer, to mingle with the jingling bells and the tinkling of the cups of the water-sellers.

Then the donkey-boys, everywhere to be found in Cairo, add much to the liveliness of the streets. Their donkeys are fine animals, usually grey and very large, and their bodies are shaved in such a manner as to leave patterns on the legs and snout, which are often coloured. The saddles are of red leather and cloth, and from them hang long tassels which swing as they canter through the streets, while the musical rattle of coloured beads and the chains of copper and brass which all donkeys wear around their necks, add their quota to the many noises of the streets, through which in a low murmur one may distinguish the drone of flies.

Among all the bustle and confusion, shimmering lights, and varied colour which constitute a Cairo street scene, the native woman passes with graceful dignity. Her features are hidden by the "bourka," or veil, which is generally worn, but her beautiful eyes fascinate; nor does the voluminous cloak she wears entirely conceal the dainty, if brilliant, clothing beneath, nor the extreme beauty of her well-shaped hands and feet.

Quite as picturesque as the life of the streets are the buildings which enclose them, and the great glory of Cairo consists of its bazaars and mosques and old-time palaces.

The streets are usually irregular in width and often winding, and are sometimes so narrow as to render driving impossible, for when Cairo was built wheeled vehicles were not in use, and space within its walls was limited. The houses are very lofty, and are built of limestone or rubble covered with white plaster, and the lower courses are often coloured in stripes of yellow, white, and red. Handsome carved doorways open from the street, and the doors are panelled in bold arabesque design, or enriched by metal studs and knockers of bronze. The windows on the ground-floor, which are usually small, are closed by a wooden or iron grating, and are placed too high in the wall for passengers to look through them, and frequently, even in the best houses, small recesses in the walls serve as shops.

The upper storeys usually project beyond the ground-floor, and are supported on corbels or brackets of stone, which also are frequently carved. This method of building has two advantages, for the projecting upper storeys afford a little shade in the streets, and at the same time give greater space to the houses without encroaching upon the already narrow thoroughfares.

These upper storeys are very picturesque, for all the windows are filled with lattice-work, and large window balconies supported on carved wooden beams project far over the street. These are called "mushrabiyehs," a name which is derived from an Arabic word which means "the place for drink." Originally they were simply small cages of plain lattice-work in which the water jars were placed to cool, but as prosperity increased and the homes of the people became more ornate, first the edges of the lattice-work were cut so as to form a pattern, and the little cages presently developed into these large balconies, which in place of simple lattice-work were enclosed by screens formed of innumerable small pieces of turned wood built up so as to form designs of great beauty, and behind which the ladies of the harīm might sit and enjoy the air and the animation of the streets unseen.

Unfortunately this beautiful work is fast disappearing; visitors have discovered how adaptable it is to home decoration, and the dealers in Cairo eagerly buy up all that can be obtained to be converted into those many articles of Arab furniture with which we are now so familiar in England.

Picturesque as all the streets of Cairo are, they are not all so animated as those I have described, and in many quarters one may ride for miles through streets so narrow that no vehicle could pass, and so silent as to appear deserted. Very often their projecting upper storeys almost touch across the street, and make it so dark as to be almost like a tunnel. The handsome doorways also are often half buried in the dÃ©bris which for three hundred years or more has been accumulating in the narrow lanes, so much so that in many cases the doors cannot be opened at all. There is an air of decay and sadness in many of these quarters, for these half ruinous houses, once the palaces of the MemlŪks, are now the habitations of the lowest of the people, and poverty and squalor reign where once had been gaiety and the fashionable life of Cairo.

CHAPTER IV
CAIRO--II

Fascinating though the streets of Cairo are, continuous sight-seeing in the heat and glare is tiring, and it is always a pleasant change to escape from the movement and bustle outside, and enjoy the quietude of some cool mosque or palace courtyard.

Having described the exterior of the native house, it will interest you to know what it is like inside. Entering from the street, one usually has to descend one or more steps to the entrance hall or passage, which, in the case of the older houses, is invariably built with at least one turning, so that no one from the street could see into the interior court or garden should the door be open, for privacy was always jealously guarded by the Mohammedans. On one side is a raised stone platform, seat for the "boab" or door-keeper, and other servants of the house. Passing through this passage, we reach the courtyard, which is often very large and open to the sky, and into which most of the windows of the house open. On one side is a large recess or bay raised slightly above the pavement of the court, and furnished with benches of carved wood. The beams of the ceiling and handsome cornice are richly ornamented with carving and illumination, and the heavy beam which spans the entrance is supported by a pillar of elegant shape and proportion. Here, or in the "mandara"[3] inside the house, the Arab host receives his male guests. On the most shady side of the court are placed the "zīrs," while several doors lead to the harīm, as the ladies' quarters are called, and the various offices and reception-rooms of the house. These doors are always panelled in elaborate geometrical designs, and the principal one, which is reached by a short flight of stone steps, is set in a lofty recess, the trefoil head of which is richly carved. This gives access to the reception-room on the first

3   Guest chamber.

floor. One side is entirely open to the air, and through three archways connected by a low balustrade of perforated stonework overlooks the court. The floor is paved in tiles or marble of various colours, usually in some large design, in the centre of which is a shallow basin in which a fountain plays. Round the three walls is a raised daīs called "lewan," covered with rugs or mattresses, on which the guests recline. Little recesses in the walls, which in the homes of the wealthy are elaborately decorated with mosaic or tile work, contain the water jars, and the "tisht wa abrīk," or water-jug and basin, used for the ceremonial washing of hands before meat. The walls are usually plain, and are only broken by the "dulab," or wall cupboard, in which pipes and other articles are kept. The ceiling is heavily beamed and illuminated, or covered with appliquÃ© work in some rich design, the spaces variously coloured or picked out in gold.

For cold weather another similar room is provided in the interior of the house much as the one I have described, but with the addition of a cupola or dome over the fountain, while the large windows, in the recesses of which couches are placed, are filled with the beautiful "mushrabiyeh" work we have noticed from the streets, or by stained glass set in perforated plaster work. These rooms contain practically no furniture, excepting the low "sahniyeh," or tray, upon which refreshments are served, and the copper brazier which contains the charcoal fire, but from the ceiling hang numbers of beautifully-wrought lamps of metal and coloured glass. We can imagine how rich a scene such a room would form when illuminated for the reception of guests whose gorgeous Oriental costumes accord so well with its handsome interior, while the finishing touch is given by the performance of the musicians and singing girls with which the guests are entertained, leading one instinctively to call to mind many similar scenes so wonderfully described in the "Arabian Nights." Many of the adventures of its heroes and heroines are suggested by the secret passages which the wall cupboards often hide, and may well have occurred in houses we may visit to-day in Cairo, for, more than any other, Cairo is the city of the "Arabian Nights," and in our walks one may at any moment meet the hunchback or the pastry-cook, or the one-eyed calender, whose adventures fills so many pages of that fascinating book; while the summary justice and drastic measures of the old khalifs are recalled by the many instruments of torture or of death which may still be seen hanging in the bazaars or from the city gates.

Everyone who goes to Cairo is astonished at the great number and beauty of its mosques, nearly every street having one or more. Altogether there are some 500 or more in Cairo, as well as a great number of lesser shrines where the people worship. I will tell you how this comes about. We have often read in the "Arabian Nights" in what a high-handed and frequently unjust manner the property of some poor unfortunate would be seized and given to another. This was very much the case in Cairo in the olden days, and khalifs and cadis, muftis and pashas, were not very scrupulous about whose money or possessions they administered, and even to-day in some Mohammedan countries it is not always wise for a man to grow rich.

And so it was that in order to escape robbery in the name of law many wealthy merchants preferred to build during their lifetime a mosque or other public build-ing, while money left for this purpose was regarded as sacred, and so the many beautiful sebīls and mosques of Cairo came into existence.

Egypt is so old that even the Roman times appear new, and one is tempted to regard these glorious buildings of the Mohammedan era as only of yesterday. Yet many of the mosques which people visit and admire are older than any church or cathedral in England. We all think of Lincoln Cathedral or Westminster Abbey as being very venerable buildings, and so they are; but long before they were built the architecture of the Mohammedans in Egypt had developed into a perfect style, and produced many of the beautiful mosques in which the Cairene prays to-day.

As a rule the mosque was also the tomb of its founder, and the dome was de-signed as a canopy over his burial-place, so that when a mosque is *domed* we know it to be the mausoleum of some great man, while the beautiful minaret or tower is common to all mosques, whether tomb-mosque or not.

One of the most striking features of a mosque is the doorway, which is placed in a deep arched recess, very lofty and highly ornamented. A flight of stone steps lead from the street to the door, which is often of hammered bronze and green with age, and from a beam which spans the recess hang curious little lamps, which are lit on fete days.

At the top of the steps is a low railing or barrier which no one may cross *shod*, for beyond this is holy ground, where, as in the old days of Scripture, every one must "put off his shoes from off his feet."

The interior of the mosque is often very rich and solemn. It is usually built in the form of a square courtyard, open to the sky, in which is the "hanafieh," or tank, where "the faithful" wash before prayers. The court is surrounded by cloisters supported by innumerable pillars, or else lofty horseshoe arches lead into deep bays or recesses, the eastern one of which, called the "kibleh," is the holiest, and corresponds to our chancel, and in the centre of the wall is the "mirhab," or niche, which is in the direction of Mecca, and the point towards which the Moslem prays.

Marble pavements, beautiful inlay of ivory and wood, stained-glass windows, and elaborately decorated ceilings and domes, beautify the interior, and go to form a rich but subdued coloured scheme, solemn and restful, and of which perhaps my picture will give you some idea.

Attached to most mosques is a sebĪl, also beautiful in design. The lower story has a fountain for the use of wayfarers; above, in a bright room open to the air, is a little school, where the boys and girls of the quarter learn to recite sundry passages from the Koran, and which until recently was practically all the education they received.

And now I must tell you something about the bazaars, which, after the mosques, are the most interesting relics in Cairo, and in many cases quite as old. First, I may say that the word "bazaar" means "bargain," and as in the East a fixed price is unusual, and anything is worth just what can be got for it, making a purchase is generally a matter of patience, and one may often spend days in acquiring some simple article of no particular value. An exception is the trade in copper ware, which is sold by weight, and it is a common practice among the poorer classes to invest their small savings in copper vessels of which they have the benefit, and which can readily be sold again should money be wanted. This trade is carried on in a very picturesque street, called the "SÃ»k-en-NahassĪn," or street of the coppersmiths, where in tiny little shops 4 or 5 feet square, most of the copper and brass industry of Cairo is carried on. Opening out of this street are other bazaars, many very ancient, and each built for some special trade. So we have the shoemaker's bazaar, the oil, spice, Persian and goldsmith's bazaars, and many others, each different in character, and generally interesting as architecture. The Persian bazaar is now nearly demolished, and the "Khan Khalili," once the centre of the carpet trade, and the most beautiful of all, is now split up into a number of small curio shops, for the people are becoming Europeanized, and the Government, alas! appear to have no interest in the preservation of buildings of great historic interest and beauty.

One other feature of old Cairo I must notice before leaving the subject. In the old days of long caravan journeys, when merchants from Persia, India, and China brought their wares to Cairo overland, it was their custom to travel in strong companies capable of resisting possible attacks by the wild desert tribes, and in Cairo special "khans," or inns, were built to accommodate the different nationalities or trades. In the central court the horses and camels of the different caravans were tethered; surrounding it, and raised several feet above the ground, were numerous bays in which the goods were exposed for sale. Above, several storeys provided sleeping accommodation for the travellers. Like the bazaars, many of these khans are very ancient, and are most interesting architecturally as well as being fast disappearing relics of days which, until the introduction of railways and steamers, perpetuated in our own time conditions of life and trade which had continued uninterruptedly since that time so long ago when Joseph first built his store cities and granaries in Egypt.

It is impossible in a few pages to convey any real impression of Cairo, and I have only attempted to describe a few of its most characteristic features. There is, however, a great deal more to see--the citadel, built by that same Saladīn against whom our crusaders fought in Palestine, and which contains many ancient mosques and other buildings of historic interest, and the curious well called Joseph's Well, where, by means of many hundreds of stone steps, the visitor descends into the heart of the rock upon which the citadel is built, and which until recently supplied it with water. Close by is the parapet from which the last of the Memlūks made his desperate leap for freedom, and became sole survivor of his class so treacherously murdered by Mohammed Ali; behind, crowning the Mokhattam Hills, is the little fort built by Napoleon the Great to command the city, while in every direction are views almost impossible of description. To the east is that glorious cemetery known as the "tombs of the khalifs," which contains many of the finest architectural gems of mediÃival Egypt; to the west is Fostat, the original "city of the tent," from which Cairo sprang, while over the rubbish heaps of old Babylon, the Roman aqueduct stretches towards Rhoda, that beautiful garden island on whose banks tradition has it that the infant Moses was found, while still further across the river, sail-dotted and gleaming in the sun, the great Pyramids mark the limit of the Nile Valley and the commencement of that enormous desert which stretches to the Atlantic Ocean. Looking south, past Memphis and the Pyramids of Sakkara and DarshŪr, the Nile loses itself in the distant heat haze, while to the north is stretched before us the fertile plains of the Delta.

At our feet lies the wonderful Arab town, whose domes and minarets rise high above the dwellings which screen the streets from view, but whose seething life is evidenced by the dull roar which reaches you even at this distance. It is a city of sunlight, rich in buildings of absorbing interest and ablaze with colour. As for the people, ignorant and noisy though they are, they have much good-humour and simple kindness in their natures, and it is worth notice that a stranger may walk about in safety in the most squalid quarters of the city, and of what European capital could this be said?

CHAPTER V
THE NILE--I

I have already told you how the land of Egypt was first formed by the river which is still its source of life; but before saying anything about the many monuments on its banks or the floating life it carries, I want you to look at the map with me for a moment, and see what we can learn of the character of the river itself.

The Nile is one of the world's *great* rivers, and is about 3,400 miles long. As you will see, it has its source in the overflow from Lake Victoria Nyanza, when it flows in a generally northern direction for many hundreds of miles, receiving several tributaries, such as the River Sobat and the Bahr-el-Ghazal, whose waters, combining with the Bahr-el-Abiad, or White Nile, as it is called, maintain the steady constant flow of the river.

Eventually it is joined by the Bahr-el-Azrak, or Blue Nile, which rises among the mountains of Abyssinia and enters the White Nile at KhartŪm.

During a great part of the year this branch is dry, but filled by the melting snow and torrential rains of early spring, the Blue Nile becomes a surging torrent, and pours its muddy water, laden with alluvial soil and forest dÃ©bris, into the main river, causing it to rise far above its ordinary level, and so bringing about that annual overflow which in Egypt takes the place of rain.

It is certain that the ancient Egyptians knew nothing as to the source of their great water-supply,[4] their knowledge being limited to the combined river which begins at KhartŪm, and for 1,750 miles flows uninterruptedly, and, with the exception of the River Atbara, without further tributaries until it reaches the sea; and it is curious to think that for every one of these 1,750 miles the Nile is a *slowly dimin-*

4   Many of the ancients believed the First Cataract to be its source.

ishing stream, water-wheels, steam-pumps, and huge arterial canals distributing its water in all directions over the land. The large number of dams and regulators constructed within recent years still further aid this distribution of the Nile water, and it is a remarkable and almost incredible fact that with the closing of the latest barrage at Damietta, the Nile will be so completely controlled that of all the flow of water which pours so magnificently through the cataracts not a drop will reach the sea!

One can easily understand the reverence with which the ancients regarded their mysterious river, which, rising no one knew where, year by year continued its majestic flow, and by its regular inundations brought wealth to the country, and it is no wonder that the rising of its waters should have been the signal for a series of religious and festal ceremonies, and led the earlier inhabitants of Egypt to worship the river as a god. Some of these festivals still continue, and it is only a very few years since the annual sacrifice of a young girl to the Nile in flood was prohibited by the Khedive.

Though regular in its period of inundation, which begins in June, its height varies from year to year; 40 to 45 feet constitutes a good Nile--anything less than this implies a shortage of water and more or less scanty crops; while should the Nile rise *higher* than 45 feet the result is often disastrous, embankments being swept away, gardens devastated, while numbers of houses and little hamlets built on the river-banks are undermined and destroyed.

The whole river as known to the ancients was navigable, and formed the great trade route by which gold from Sheba, ivory, gum, ebony, and many other commodities were brought into the country. The armies of Pharaoh were carried by it on many warlike expeditions, and by its means the Roman legions penetrated to the limits of the then known world.

Hippopotamus and crocodile were numerous, and afforded sport for the nobles, and though steamboats and increased traffic have driven these away, on many a temple wall are pictured incidents of the chase, as well as records of their wars.

It is natural, therefore, that on the banks of their mighty waterway the Egyptians should have erected their greatest monuments, and the progress of the Roman armies may still be traced by the ruins of their fortified towns and castles, which, from many a rocky islet or crag, command the river.

In another chapter I will tell you more about the monuments; at present I wish to describe the Nile as it appears to-day.

Our first view of the river is obtained as we cross the Kasr-en-Nil bridge at Cairo to join one of the many steamers by which visitors make the Nile trip, and one's first impression is one of great beauty, especially in the early morning. On the East Bank the old houses of Būlak rise from the water's edge, and continue in a series of old houses and palaces to the southern end of Rhoda Island, whose tall palms and cypress-trees rise above the silvery mist which still hangs upon the water. On the west the high mud-banks are crowned with palms and lebbek-trees as far as one can see. Below the bridge, their white sails gleaming in the early sun, hundreds of Nile boats are waiting in readiness for the time appointed for its opening. On both banks steady streams of people pass to and fro to fill their water-skins or jars, while children paddle in the stream or make mud-pies upon the bank as they will do all the world over.

The water is very muddy and very smooth, and reflects every object to perfection; for these early mornings are almost invariably still, and the water is unruffled by the north wind, which, with curious regularity, springs up before midday.

I have already spoken of the high lateen sail of the Nile boats, a form of sail which, though beautiful, has not been devised for *pictorial* purposes. In every country and in every sea peculiarities of build and rig are displayed in native vessels. This is not the result of whim or chance, but has been evolved as the result of long experience of local requirements and conditions, and in every case I think it may be taken that the native boat is the one most suited to the conditions under which it is employed. So on the Nile these lofty sails are designed to overtop the high banks and buildings, and so catch the breeze which would otherwise be intercepted. The build of the boats also is peculiar; they are very wide and flat bottomed, and the rudders are unusually large, so as to enable them to turn quickly in the narrow channels, which are often tortuous. The bow rises in a splendid curve high out of the water, and throws the spray clear of its low body, for the Egyptian loads his boat very heavily, and I have often seen them so deep in the water that a little wall of mud has been added to the gunwale so as to keep out the waves.

These native boats are of several kinds, from the small "felucca," or open boat used for ferry or pleasure purposes, to the large "giassa," or cargo boat of the river.

Some of these are very large, carrying two or three enormous sails, while their cargoes of coal or goods of various kinds are often as much as 150 tons; yet they sail fast, and with a good breeze there are few steamers on the river which could beat them.

The navigation of the Nile is often difficult, especially when the river is falling, for each year it alters its course and new sand-banks are formed, and it is not always easy to decide which is the right channel to steer for. The watermen, however, are very expert, and can usually determine their course by the nature of the ripple on the water, which varies according to its depth. Frequently, however, from accidents of light or other causes, it is not possible to gauge the river in this way, so every boat is provided with long sounding-poles called "midra," by means of which men stationed at either side of the bow feel their way through the difficult channels, calling out the depths of water as they go. In spite of these precautions, however, steamers and sailing boats alike often stick fast upon some bank which has, perhaps, been formed in a few hours by a sudden shift of the wind or slight diversion of the current, caused by the tumbling in of a portion of the bank a little higher up-stream. Many of these boats travel long distances, bringing cargoes of coal, cement, machinery, cotton goods, and hardware from the coast for distribution in the provinces of Upper Egypt, and on their return voyage are laden with sugar-cane or corn, and many other articles of produce and native manufacture. As night falls, they usually moor alongside the bank, when fires are lit, and the crews prepare their simple evening meal. The supply of food, it may be noticed, is usually kept in a bag, which is slung from the rigging, or a short post where all can see it and no one be able to take advantage of another by feeding surreptitiously.

It is often a pretty sight when several of these boats are moored together, when, their day's work over, their crews will gather round the fires, and to the accompaniment of tambourine or drum sing songs or recite stories until it is time to sleep. No sleeping accommodation is provided, and all the hardy boatman does is to wrap his cloak about his head and lie among whatever portion of the cargo is least hard and offers most protection from the wind.

The Nile banks themselves are interesting. In colour and texture rather like chocolate, they are cut into terraces by the different levels of the water, while the lapping of the waves is perpetually undermining them, so that huge slabs of the rich alluvial mud are continually falling away into the river. Each of these terraces, as it emerges from the receding water, is planted with beans or melons by the thrifty farmer, while the sand-banks forming in the river will presently also be under cultivation, the natives claiming them while still covered with water, their claims being staked by Indian-corn stalks or palm-branches.

Like the canal banks in the Delta, the Nile banks form the great highway for Upper Egypt, and at all times of the day one may see the people and their animals silhouetted against the sky as they pass to and fro between their villages. In the neighbourhood of large towns, or such villages as hold a weekly market, the banks are very animated, and for many miles are thronged with people from the surrounding district, some walking, others riding on camels, donkeys, or buffaloes, pressing towards the market to enjoy the show, or sell the many articles of produce with which they are laden.

At the water's edge herds of buffaloes wallow in the river, tended by a little boy who stares stolidly at your steamer as it passes or, in great excitement, chases your vessel and vainly cries for "backshish."[5] At frequent intervals are the water-wheels and "shadŪfs," which raise the water to the level of the fields, and these are such important adjuncts of the farm that I must describe them. The "shadŪf" is one of the oldest and one of the simplest methods of raising water in existence. A long pole is balanced on a short beam supported by two columns of mud, about 4 or 5 feet high, erected at the end of the water channel to be supplied; 6 feet or more below it is the pool or basin cut in the river-bank, and which is kept supplied with water by a little channel from the river. One end of the pole is weighted by a big lump of mud; from the other a leather bucket is suspended by means of a rope of straw, or a second and lighter pole. In order to raise the water, the shadŪf worker, bending his weight upon the rope, lowers the bucket into the basin below, which, when filled, is easily raised by the balancing weight, and is emptied into the channel above. As the river falls the basin can no longer be fed by the river, so a second "shadŪf" is erected in order to keep the first supplied, and in low Nile it is quite a common sight to see four of these "shadŪfs," one above the other, employed in raising the water from the river-level to the high bank above. This work is, perhaps, the most arduous of any farm labour, and the workers are almost entirely naked as they toil in the

---

5   "A gift."

sun, while a screen of cornstalks is often placed to protect them from the cold north wind. The water-wheels, or "sakia," as they are called, are of two kinds, and both ingenious. Each consists of a large wheel placed horizontally, which is turned by one or more bullocks; the spokes of this wheel project as cogs, so as to turn another wheel placed below it at right angles. When used in the fields, the rim of this second wheel is hollow and divided into segments, each with a mouth or opening. As the wheel revolves its lower rim is submerged in the well, filling its segments with water, which, as they reach the top, empty their contents sideways into a trough, which carries the water to the little "genena," or watercourse, which supplies the fields. Those used on the river-bank, however, are too far from the water for such a wheel to be of use, so in place of the hollow rim the second wheel also has cogs, on which revolves an endless chain of rope to which earthen pots are attached, and whose length may be altered to suit the varying levels of the river. Some of these "sakias" are very pretty, as they are nearly always shaded by trees of some kind as a protection to the oxen who work them.

One of the prettiest incidents of all, however, is the village watering-place, where morning and evening the women and children of the town congregate to fill their water-pots, wash their clothing or utensils, and enjoy a chat. It is pretty to watch them as they come and go; often desperately poor, they wear their ragged, dust-soiled clothing with a queenly grace, for their lifelong habit of carrying burdens upon their heads, and their freedom from confining garments, have given them a carriage which women in this country might well envy. Though generally dark-skinned and toil-worn, many of the younger women are beautiful, while all have shapely and delicately-formed limbs, and eyes and teeth of great beauty. At the water's edge the children are engaged in scrubbing cooking-pots and other utensils, while their elders are employed in washing their clothing or domestic linen, when, after perhaps enjoying a bathe themselves, their water-pots are filled, and, struggling up the steep bank, they disappear towards the village. These water-pots, by the way, are two-handled, and pretty in shape, and are always slightly conical at the base, so that they are able to stand on the shelving river-banks without falling, and for the same reason are nearly always carried slightly sideways on the head. It is pretty to see the wonderful sense of balance these girls display in carrying their water-pots, which they seldom touch with their hand, and it is surprising also what great weights even young girls are able to support, for a "balass" filled with water is often a load too heavy for her to raise to her head without the assistance of another. Like all the poor, they are always obliging to each other, and I recently witnessed a pathetic sight at one of these village watering-places, when an old woman, too infirm to carry her "balass" herself, was with difficulty struggling down the bank and leading a blind man, who bore her burden for her.

CHAPTER VI
THE NILE--II

The Nile varies considerably in width, from a quarter of a mile, as in the deep channel before Cairo, to two miles or more higher up, where the wide space between its high banks, filled to the brim during high Nile, has almost the appearance of a sea; but as the river falls it is studded with islands, many of them of considerable extent, and often under permanent cultivation. The navigable channel is close under one bank or other, though the shallow water which covers the shoals gives the river the appearance of being considerably larger than it really is. In character the scenery is generally placid, and the smooth water, shimmering under the warm sun which edges the sand-banks with a gleaming line of silver, is hardly broken by a ripple. I always think the river prettiest when the Nile is low and the sand-banks appear. In the shallows pelicans, ibis, heron, and stork are fishing together without interfering with each other, while large flights of wild-duck rise splashing from the stream. Eagles soar aloft, or, with the vultures, alight upon a sand-bank to dispute the possession of some carcass with the jackals and the foxes. Water wag-tails flit along the shore, or in the most friendly manner board your steamer to feed on the crumbs from your tea-table, while large numbers of gay-plumaged king-fishers dart in and out from their nests tunnelled far into the precipitous face of the river-bank.

On either side are the eternal hills, beautiful under any effect of light.

It is astonishing how infinitely varied the Nile scenery is according to the time of day. In the early morning, mists often hang upon the water, and the air is bitterly cold, for these sandy wastes which abut upon the Nile retain little heat by night. Above the cool green of the banks the high hills rise mysteriously purple against the sunrise, or catch the first gleam of gold on their rugged bluffs.

As the sun mounts higher a delicate pink tinge suffuses all, and the hanging mists are dispersed by the growing heat to form little flecks of white which float in the deep blue of the sky above you. Meanwhile the life of the river and the fields has recommenced, and the banks again become animated, and innumerable Nile boats dot the surface of the stream.

At midday the landscape is enveloped in a white heat, while the bluffs and buttresses of the rocks cast deep purple shadows on the sweeping sand-drifts which lie against their base. It is a drowsy effect of silver and grey, when Nature seems asleep and man and beast alike are inclined to slumber.

Towards evening, glorified by the warm lights, how rich in colour the scenery becomes! The western banks, crowned by dense masses of foliage, whose green appears almost black against the sunset, are reflected in the water below, its dark surface broken by an occasional ripple and little masses of foam which have drifted down from the cataract hundreds of miles away. Beyond the belt of trees the minarets of some distant village are clear cut against the sky, for the air is so pure that distance seems to be annihilated. Looking east, the bold cliffs face the full glory of the sunset, and display a wonderful transformation of colour, as the white or biscuit-coloured rocks reflect the slowly changing colour of the light. They gradually become enveloped in a ruddy glow, in which the shadows of projections appear an aerial blue, and seem to melt imperceptibly into the glowing sky above them. Gradually a pearly shadow creeps along the base of the cliffs or covers the whole range, and one would suppose that the glory of the sunset was past. In about a quarter of an hour, however, commences the most beautiful transformation of all, and one which I think is peculiar to the Nile Valley, for a second glow, more beautiful and more ethereal than the first, overspreads the hills, which shine like things translucent against the purple earth-shadow which slowly mounts in the eastern sky. The sails of the boats on the river meanwhile have taken on a tint like old ivory, while perhaps a full moon appears above the hill-tops, and in twisting bars of silver is reflected in the gently moving water at your feet.

The Nile is not always in so gentle a mood as this, however, for on most days a strong north wind disturbs the water, and changes the placid river into one of sparkling animation. The strong wind, meeting the current of the stream, breaks the water into waves which are foam-flecked and dash against the muddy cliffs and sand-banks, while the quickly sailing boats bend to the wind, and from their bluff and brightly-painted bows toss the sprays high into the air, or turn the water from their sides in a creamy cataract. The sky also is flecked with rounded little wind-clouds, whose undersides are alternately grey or orange as they pass over the cultivated land or desert rock, whose colour they partially reflect. The colour of the water also becomes very varied, for the turn of each wave reflects something of the blue sky above, and the sun shines orange through the muddy water as it curls, while further variety of tint is given by the passing cloud-shadows and the intense blueness of the smoother patches which lie upon the partially covered sand-spits. This always forms a gay scene, for the river is crowded with vessels which sail quickly, and take every advantage of the favourable wind. Sometimes the north wind becomes dangerous in its energy, and wrecks are not infrequent, while from the south-west, at certain periods of the year, comes the hot "khamsīn" wind, which, lashing the water into fury, and filling the air with dust, renders navigation almost impossible.

Some of the cargoes carried by these Nile boats are worth describing, and large numbers are employed in carrying "tibbin" from the farms to the larger towns. "Tibbin" is the chopped straw upon which horses and cattle in the towns are mainly fed, and it is loaded on to the boats in a huge pyramidical pile carried upon planks which considerably overhang the boat's sides. The steersman is placed upon the top of this stack, and is enabled to guide his vessel by a long pole lashed to the tiller, and it is curious to notice that the "tibbin," though finely chopped, does not appear to blow away.

In a somewhat similar manner the immense quantity of balass and other water-pots, which are manufactured at Girgeh, Sohag, and other places on the Upper Nile, are transported down-stream. In this case, however, large beams of wood are laid across the boats, which are often loaded in couples lashed together, and from which are slung nets upon which the water-pots are piled to the height of 10 or 12 feet, and one may often meet long processions of these boats slowly drifting down stream to Assiut or Cairo.

Another frequent cargo is sugar-cane, perhaps the greatest industry of the upper river, and at Manfalut, Rhoda, Magaga, and many other places large sugar factories have sprung into existence of late years. The trade is a very profitable one for

Egypt, but, unfortunately, their tall chimneys and ugly factories, which are always built close to the Nile bank, are doing much to spoil the beauties of the river, and, worst of all, noisy little steam tugs and huge iron barges are yearly becoming more numerous.

Though, as we have seen, crocodiles have long ago left the Lower Nile, the river abounds in fish, and from the terraces of its banks one may constantly see fishermen throwing their hand-nets, while in the shallows and backwaters of the river, drag-nets are frequently employed. I recently watched the operation, which I will describe. Beginning at the lower end of the reach, seven men were employed in working the net, three at either end to haul it, while another, wading in the middle, supported it at the centre. Meanwhile two of their party had run far up the banks, one on either side, and then, entering the water, slowly descended towards the nets, shouting and beating the water with sticks, thus driving the fish towards the nets. Usually the fish so caught are small, or of only moderate size, though I have frequently seen exposed for sale in the markets fish weighing upwards of 300 pounds and 6 feet or more in length.

The Nile Valley is comparatively wide for a considerable distance above Cairo, and while the hills which fringe the Lybian desert are generally in view in the distance, those on the eastern side gradually close in upon the river as we ascend, and in many places, such as Gibel Kasr-es-Saad, or "the castle of the hunter," Feshun, or Gibel Abou Fedr, rise almost perpendicularly from the river to the height of 1,000 feet or more, and although considerable areas of cultivated land are to be found at intervals on the eastern side, practically all the agricultural land of Upper Egypt lies on the western bank of the river.

The rock of which the hills are formed is limestone, and it is a very dazzling sight as you pass some of these precipitous cliffs in the brilliant sunshine, especially where the quarrymen are working and the sunburnt outside has been removed, exposing the pure whiteness of the stone.

Along the narrow bank of shingle at the foot of the cliffs flocks of dark-coated sheep and goats wander in search of such scant herbage as may be found along the water's edge, and many native boats lie along the banks loading the stone extracted by the quarrymen, who look like flies on the face of the rock high above you. Enormous quantities of stone are required for the building of the various dams and locks on the river, as well as for the making of embankments and "spurs." These "spurs" are little embankments which project into the river at a slight angle pointing down-stream, and are made in order to turn the direction of the current towards the middle of the river, and so protect the banks from the scour of the water; for each year a portion of the banks is lost, and in many places large numbers of palm-trees and dwellings are swept away, for the native seems incapable of learning how un-wise it is to build at the water's edge. Sometimes whole fields are washed away by the flood, and the soil, carried down-stream, forms a new island, or is perhaps de-posited on the opposite side of the river many miles below. When this occurs, the new land so formed is held to be the property of the farmer or landowner who has suffered loss.

These changes of the river-banks are often rapid. One year vessels may dis-charge their passengers or cargoes upon the bank whereon some town or village is built, and which the following year may be separated from the river by fields many acres in extent; and each year in going up the Nile one may notice striking changes in this way.

As the Nile winds in its course the rocky hills on either side alternately ap-proach close to the river, revealing a succession of rock-hewn tombs or ancient monasteries, or recede far into the distance, half hidden in the vegetation of the ar-able land; but, speaking generally, the river flows principally on the eastern side of the valley, while all the large towns, such as Wasta, Minyeh, Assiut, or Girgeh are built upon the western bank, where the largest area of fertility is situated.

As we ascend the river the vegetation slowly changes; cotton and wheat, so freely grown in the Delta, give place to sugar-cane and Indian corn, and the feath-ery foliage of the sunt and mimosa trees is more in evidence than the more richly clad lebbek or sycamore.

In many places are fields of the large-leaved castor-oil plants, whose crimson flower contrasts with the delicately tinted blossoms of the poppies which, for the sake of their opium, are grown upon the shelving banks. The dÃ´m palm also is a new growth, and denotes our approach to tropical regions, while the type and costume of the people have undergone a change, for they are darker and broader in feature than the people of Lower Egypt, and the prevailing colour of their clothing is a dark brown, the natural colour of their sheep, from whose wool their heavy homespun cloth is made.

The limestone hills which have been our companions since leaving Cairo also disappear, and a little way above Luxor low hills of sandstone closely confine the river in a very narrow channel. This is the Gibel Silsileh, which from the earliest times has supplied the stone of which the temples are built. These celebrated quarries produce the finest stone in the country, and have always been worked in the most scientific and methodical manner, deep cuttings following the veins of good stone which only was extracted, while the river front has remained practically untouched--a contrast to the modern method of quarrying, where the most striking bluffs upon the Nile are being recklessly blown away, causing an enormous waste of material as well as seriously affecting the beauty of the scenery.

CHAPTER VII
THE NILE--III

After a river journey of 583 miles from Cairo, Assuan is reached--limit of Egypt proper and the beginning of an entirely new phase of Nile scenery. Cultivation in any large sense has been left behind, and we are now in Nubia, a land of rock and sand, sparsely inhabited, and, excepting in very small patches along the water's edge, producing no crops.

Built at the northern end of what is called the first cataract, Assuan is perhaps the most interesting and prettily-situated town in Upper Egypt. Facing the green island of Elephantine and the golden sand-drifts which cover the low range of hills across the river, Assuan stretches along the river-bank, its white buildings partly screened by the avenue of palms and lebbek-trees which shade its principal street, while to the north are dense groves of date-palms, past which the Nile sweeps in a splendid curve and is lost to sight among the hills. Behind, beyond its open-air markets and the picturesque camp of the Besharīn, the desert stretches unbroken to the shores of the Red Sea.

The bazaars of Assuan are extremely picturesque, and are covered almost throughout their length; the lanes which constitute them are narrow and winding, forming enticing vistas whose distances are emphasized by the occasional glints of sunlight which break in upon their generally subdued light. In the shops are exposed for sale all those various goods and commodities which native life demands; but visitors are mostly attracted by the stalls of the curio sellers, who display a strange medley of coloured beads and baskets, rich embroideries, stuffed animals, and large quantities of arms and armour, so-called trophies of the wars in the SŪdan. Though most of these relics are spurious, genuine helmets and coats of mail of old Persian and Saracenic times may occasionally be found, while large numbers of spears and swords are undoubtedly of Dervish manufacture.

For most Englishmen Assuan has also a tragic interest in its association with the expedition for the relief of General Gordon, and the subsequent Mahdist wars, when regiment after regiment of British soldiers passed through her streets on their way towards those burning deserts from which so many of them were destined never to return. Those were exciting, if anxious, days for Assuan, and many visitors will remember how, some years ago, the presence of Dervish horsemen in its immediate vicinity rendered it unsafe for them to venture outside the town. Those days are happily over, and there is now little use for the Egyptian forts which to the south and east guarded the little frontier town.

From a ruined Roman fort which crowns a low hill at the south end of the town we have our first view of the cataract, and the sudden change in the character of the scenery is remarkable.

In place of the broad fields and mountains to which we have been accustomed, the river here flows in a basin formed by low, precipitous hills, and is broken by innumerable rocky islets on different levels, which form the series of rapids and little cascades which give the cataract its name. These little islets are formed by a collection of boulders of red granite filled in with silt, and have a very strange effect, for the boulders are rounded by the action of the water, which, combined with the effect of the hot sun, has caused the red stone to become coated with a hard skin, black and smooth to touch, just as though they had been blackleaded.

Many of the islets are simply rocks of curious shapes which jut out of the water; others are large enough to be partially cultivated, and their little patches of green are peculiarly vivid in contrast with the rock and sand which form their setting.

The scenery is wildly fantastic, for while the rocks which form the western bank are almost entirely covered by the golden sand-drifts which pour over them, smooth as satin, to the water's edge, those on the east are sun-baked and forbidding, a huge agglomeration of boulders piled one upon the other and partially covered by shingle, which crackle under foot like clinkers; between are the islands, many crowned by a hut or pigeon-cote, and with their greenery often perfectly reflected in the rapidly flowing water.

Though navigation here is difficult, and a strong breeze is necessary to enable vessels to ascend the river, boat sailing is a popular feature of European life in Assuan, a special kind of sailing-boat being kept for visitors, who organize regattas and enjoy many a pleasant picnic beneath the shade of the dÃ´m palms or mimosa-trees which grow among the rocks.

In the old days the great excursion from Assuan was by water to the "Great Gate," as the principal rapid was called, often a difficult matter to accomplish. To-day the great dam has replaced it as the object of a sail.

This is the greatest engineering work of the kind ever constructed, and spans the Nile Valley at the head of the cataract basin. It is a mile and a quarter in length, and the river, which is raised in level about 66 feet, pours through a great number of sluice-gates which are opened or shut according to the season of the year and the necessities of irrigation or navigation.

Behind, the steep valley is filled, and forms a huge lake extending eighty miles to the south, and many pretty villages have been submerged, while of the date-groves which surrounded them the crests of the higher trees alone appear above water. The green island of PhilÃ¦ also is engulfed, and of the beautiful temple of Isis built upon it only the upper portion is visible.

Below the dam activity of many kinds characterizes the Nile, as does the sound of rushing water the Cataract basin. Above, silence reigns, for the huge volume of stored water lies inert between its rugged banks.

One's first thought is one of sadness, for everywhere the tree-tops, often barely showing above water, seem to mourn the little villages and graveyards which lie below, and as yet no fresh verdure has appeared to give the banks the life and beauty they formerly had.

As at the cataract, here also the hills are simply jumbled heaps of granite boulders, fantastically piled one upon the other, barren and naked, and without any vegetable growth to soften their forbidding wildness.

On many rocky islands are the ruined mud buildings of the Romans, and more than one village, once populous, lies deserted and abandoned upon some promontory which is now surrounded by the flood.

Though a general sense of mournfulness pervades it, the scenery has much variety and beauty, nor have all the villages been destroyed; many had already been built far above the present water-level, while others have sprung up to take the place of those submerged. These again present new features to the traveller, for, unlike many we have seen below the cataract, these Nubian dwellings are well built, the mud walls being neatly smoothed and often painted. The roofs are peculiar, being in the form of well-constructed semicircular arches, all of mud, and in many cases the tops of the outside walls are adorned by a kind of balustrade of open brickwork.

Half hidden among the rocks the native house has often the appearance of some temple pylon, and seems to fit the landscape in a peculiar way, for no form of building harmonizes so well with the Egyptian scenery as the temple. Whether or not the native unconsciously copies the ancient structure I cannot say, but anyone visiting Egypt must often be struck by the resemblance, particularly when, as is often the case, the little house is surmounted by pigeon-cotes, which in form are so like the temple towers.

Like their homes, the inhabitants of Nubia also differ from those of Egypt proper, for they are Berbers and more of the Arab type, handsome, and with regular features and ruddy in complexion, while many of the small children, who, excepting for a few strings of beads, run about naked, are extremely beautiful. There is one curious fact about these villages which no one could fail to notice, for while there are always plenty of women and children to be seen, there are no *men*, and though practically there is no cultivation, food appears to be abundant!

The reason is that these people are so nice in character and generally so trustworthy, that the men are all employed in Cairo and elsewhere as domestic servants, or "syces,"[6] and though they themselves may not see their homes for years, their wages are good, and so they are able to send food and clothing in plenty to their families.

As we ascend the river and approach the limit of the stored water, the banks again become fertile, for here the water is simply maintained at flood-level, and has not had the same disastrous effect as lower down the valley. Here the scenery is very striking; bold rocks jut out from the beautiful golden sand-drifts which often pour into the river itself, or in sharp contrast terminate in the brilliant line of green which fringes the banks. All around, their ruggedness softened in the warm light, are the curious, conical mountains of Nubia, and on the eastern side large groves of palms, green fields, and water-wheels make up as pretty a scene as any in Egypt;

6   Grooms.

presently, no doubt, cultivation will again appear on the barren margins of the lake above the dam and restore to it the touch of beauty it formerly had.

It is intended still further to raise the dam, and the higher level of water then maintained will not only entirely submerge PhilÃ¦, but practically all the villages now existing on its banks, as well as partially inundating many interesting temples of Roman origin. It seems a pity that so beautiful a temple as PhilÃ¦ should be lost, and one feels sorry that the villages and palm-groves of Nubia should be destroyed, but necessity knows no law, and each year water is required in greater quantities, as the area of cultivation below extends, while the villagers are amply compensated by the Government for their loss.

It is interesting to stand upon the dam and see the pent-up water pour through the sluices to form huge domes of hissing water which toss their sprays high into the air, and whose roar may be heard many miles away, while on the rocky islands down-stream numbers of natives are watching the rushing stream, ready to dive in and secure the numbers of fish of various sizes which are drawn through the sluice-gates and are stunned or killed under the great pressure of water.

There are many other interests in Assuan, which is a delightful place to visit. The desert rides, the ancient quarries where the temple obelisks were hewn, the camp of the beautiful BesharÃn, and the weirdly pictorial Cufic cemetery which winds so far along the barren valley in which the river once flowed--each have their attraction, which varies with the changing light, while many a happy hour may be spent in watching the many coloured lizards which play among the rocks, the curious mantis and twig-insects, and other strange specimens of insect life which abound here; while, should you weary of sight-seeing and the glare of light, quietude and repose may be found among the fruit-laden fig-trees of Kitchener's Island, or in the shady gardens of Elephantine.

Such in brief is the Nile from Cairo to the first cataract, though a great deal more might be written on this subject. The various towns and villages passed are often very pretty, and some are of great age, and surrounded by very interesting remains. Then there is the enjoyment of the many excursions on donkey-back to visit some tomb or temple, the amusement of bargaining for trophies or curios at the various landing-places, and a host of other interests which go to make the trip up the Nile one of the most fascinating possible, and which prevent any weariness of mind in the passenger. But to write fully about all these things is beyond the scope of this small book, though some day, perhaps, many of my readers may have the opportunity of seeing it all for themselves, and so fill in the spaces my short narrative must necessarily leave.

CHAPTER VIII
THE MONUMENTS

If asked to name any one thing which more than any other typified Egypt, the average boy or girl would at once reply, "The pyramids," and rightly, for though pyramids have been built in other countries, this particular form of structure has always been regarded as peculiarly Egyptian, and was selected by the designers of its first postage stamp as the emblem of the country.

In speaking of the pyramids it is always the pyramids of Ghizeh which are meant, for though there are a great many other pyramids in Egypt these are the largest, and being built upon the desert plateau, form such a commanding group that they dominate the landscape for miles around. All visitors to Egypt, moreover, are not able to go up the Nile or become acquainted with the temples, but everyone sees the pyramids and sphinx, which are close to Cairo, and easily reached by electric car, so to the great majority of people who visit the country they represent not only the antiquity of Egypt, but of the world.

The great pyramid of Cheops, though commenced in 3733 B.C., is not the oldest monument in Egypt; the step pyramid of Sakkara is of earlier date, while the origin of the sphinx is lost in obscurity. The pyramid, however, is of immense size, and leaves an abiding impression upon the minds of everyone who has seen it, or climbed its rugged sides. Figures convey little, I am afraid, but when I tell you that each of its sides was originally 755 feet in length and its height 481 feet, or 60 feet higher than the cross of St. Paul's, and that gangs of men, 100,000 in each, were engaged for twenty years in its construction, some idea of its immensity may be formed. At one time the pyramids were covered with polished stone, but this has all been removed and has been used in building the mosques of Cairo, and to-day its exterior is a series of steps, each 4 to 6 feet in height, formed by the enormous blocks of limestone of which it is built.

Designed as a tomb, it has various interior chambers and passages, but it was long ago ransacked by the Persians, and later by the Romans and Arabs, so that of whatever treasure it may once have contained, nothing now remains but the huge stone sarcophagus or coffin of the King.

The second pyramid, built by Chephron 3666 B.C., is little less in size, and still has a little of the outer covering at its apex. All around these two great pyramids are grouped a number of others, while the rock is honeycombed with tombs, and practically from here to the first cataract the belt of rocky hills which rise so abruptly from the Nile Valley is one continuous cemetery, only a small portion of which has so far been explored.

Close by is the sphinx, the oldest of known monuments. Hewn out of the solid rock, its enormous head and shoulders rise above the sand which periodically buries it, and, battered though it has been by Mohammed Ali's artillery, the expression of its face, as it gazes across the fertile plain towards the sunrise, is one of calm inscrutability, difficult to describe, but which fascinates the beholder.

From the plateau on which these pyramids are built may be seen successively the pyramids of AbousÍr, Sakkara, and DarshŪr, and far in the distance the curious and lonely pyramid of MedŪn. These are all built on the edge of the desert, which impinges on the cultivated land so abruptly that it is almost possible to stand with one foot in the desert and the other in the fields.

In addition to the pyramids, Sakkara has many tombs of the greatest interest, two of which I will describe.

One is called the "Serapeum," or tomb of the bulls. Here, each in its huge granite coffin, the mummies of the sacred bulls, for so long worshipped at Memphis, have been buried.

The tomb consists of a long gallery excavated in the rock below ground, on either side of which are recesses just large enough to contain the coffins, each of which is composed of a single block of stone 13 feet by 11 by 8, and which, with their contents, must have been of enormous weight, and yet they have been lowered into position in the vaults without damage. The tomb, however, was rifled long ago, and all the sarcophagi are now empty. There is one very curious fact about this tomb which I must mention, for though below ground it is so intensely hot that the heat and glare of the desert as you emerge appears relatively cool.

While the Serapeum is a triumph of engineering, the neighbouring tomb of Thi is of rare beauty, for though its design is simple, the walls, which are of fine limestone, are covered by panels enclosing carvings in low relief, representing every kind of agricultural pursuits, as well as fishing and hunting scenes. The carving is exquisitely wrought, while the various animals depicted--wild fowl, buffaloes, antelopes, or geese--are perfect in drawing and true in action.

Close to Sakkara are the dense palm-groves of Bedrashen, which surround and cover the site of ancient Memphis. At one time the most important of Egypt's capitals, Memphis has almost completely disappeared into the soft and yielding earth, and little trace of the former city now remains beyond a few stones and the colossal statue of Rameses II., one of the oppressors of Israel, which now lies prostrate and broken on the ground.

Though there have been many ancient cities in the Delta, little of them now remains to be seen, for the land is constantly under irrigation, and in course of time most of their heavy stone buildings have sunk into the soft ground and become completely covered by deposits of mud. So, as at Memphis, all that now remains of ancient Heliopolis, or On, is one granite obelisk, standing alone in the fields; while at other places, such as Tamai or BÊte-el-Haga near MansŪrah, practically nothing now remains above ground.

In Upper Egypt, where arable land was scarce and the desert close at hand, the temples have generally been built on firmer foundations, and many are still in a very perfect state of preservation, though the majority were ruined by the great earthquake of 27 B.C.

The first temple visited on the Nile trip is Dendereh, in itself perhaps not of the greatest historical value, as it is only about 2,000 years of age, which for Egypt is quite modern; but it has two points of interest for all. First, its association with Cleopatra, who, with her son, is depicted on the sculptured walls; and, secondly, because it is in such a fine state of preservation that the visitor receives a very real idea of what an Egyptian temple was like.

First let me describe the general plan of a temple; it is usually approached by a series of gateways called pylons or pro-pylons, two lofty towers with overhanging cornices, between which is the gate itself, and by whose terrace they are connected. Between these different pylons is generally a pro-naos, or avenue of sphinxes, which, on either side, face the causeway which leads to the final gate which gives entrance to the temple proper. In front of the pylons were flag-staffs, and the lofty obelisks (one of which now adorns the Thames Embankment) inscribed with deeply-cut hieroglyphic writing glorifying the King, whose colossal statues were often placed between them.

Each of the gateways, and the walls of the temple itself, are covered with inscriptions, which give it a very rich effect, their strong shadows and reflected lights breaking up the plain surface of the walls in a most decorative way, and giving colour to their otherwise plain exterior. Another point worth notice is that this succession of gateways becomes gradually larger and more ornate, so that those entering are impressed with a growing sense of wonder and admiration, which is not lessened on their return when the diminishing size of the towers serves to accentuate the idea of distance and immensity.

One of the striking features in the structure of these buildings is that while the inside walls of tower or temple are perpendicular, the outside walls are sloping. This was intended to give stability to the structure, which in modern buildings is imparted by their buttresses; but in the case of the temples it has a further value in that it adds greatly to the feeling of massive dignity which was the main principle of their design.

Entering the temple we find an open courtyard surrounded by a covered colonnade, the pillars often being made in the form of statues of its founder. This court, which is usually large, and open to the sky, was designed to accommodate the large concourse of people which would so often assemble to witness some gorgeous temple service, and beyond, through the gloomy but impressive hypostyle[7] hall, lay the shrine of the god or goddess to whom the temple was dedicated and the dark corridors and chambers in which the priests conducted their mystic rites.

In a peculiar way the temple of Dendereh impresses with a sense of mystic dignity, for though the pylons and obelisks have gone, and its outside precincts are smothered in a mass of Roman dÃ©bris, the hypostyle hall which we enter is perhaps more impressive than any other interior in Egypt. The massive stone roof, decorated with illumination and its celebrated zodiac, is supported by eighteen huge

---

7   One with a roof supported by columns.

columns, each capped by the head of the goddess Hathor, to whom the temple is dedicated, while columns and walls alike are covered with decorative inscriptions.

Through the mysterious gloom we pass through lofty doorways, which lead to the shrine or the many priests' chambers, which, entirely dark, open from the corridors.

Though it has been partially buried for centuries, and the smoke of gipsy fires has blackened much of its illuminated vault, enough of the original colour by which columns and architraves were originally enriched still remains to show us how gorgeous a building it once had been. There are a great many temples in Egypt of greater importance than Dendereh, but though Edfu, for example, is quite as perfect and much larger, it has not quite the same fascination. Others are more beautiful perhaps, and few Greek temples display more grace of ornament than Kom Ombo or submerged PhilÃ¦, while the simple beauty of Luxor or the immensity of the ruins of Karnac impress one in a manner quite different from the religious feeling inspired by gloomy Dendereh.

I have previously spoken of the hum of bees in the fields, but here we find their nests; for plastered over the cornice, and filling a large portion of the deeply-cut inscriptions, are the curious mud homes of the wild bees, who work on industriously, regardless of the attacks of the hundreds of bee-eaters[8] which feed upon them. Bees are not the only occupants of the temple, however, for swallows, pigeons, and owls nest in their quiet interiors, and the dark passages and crypts are alive with bats.

There are many other temples in Egypt of which I would like to tell you had I room to do so, but you may presently read more about them in books specially devoted to this subject. At present I want to say a few words about *hieroglyphs*, which I have frequently mentioned.

Hieroglyphic writing is really *picture* writing, and is the oldest means man has employed to enable him to communicate with his fellows. We find it in the writing of the Chinese and Japanese, among the cave-dwellers of Mexico, and the Indian tribes of North America; but the hieroglyphs of ancient Egypt differed from the others in this respect, that they had *two* values, one the *sound* value of letters or syllables of which a word was composed, the other the *picture* value which determined it; thus we find the word "cat" or "dog" spelled by two or three signs which

---

8   A small bird about the size of a sparrow.

give the letters, followed by a picture of the animal itself, so that there might be no doubt as to its meaning. This sounds quite simple, but the writing of the ancient Egyptians had developed into a grammatical system so difficult that it was only the discovery of the Rosetta stone, which was written in both hieroglyph and Greek, that gave the scholars of the world their first clue as to its meaning, and many years elapsed before the most learned of them were finally able to determine the alphabet and grammar of the early Egyptians.

I have said nothing about the religion of the Egyptians, because there were so many different deities worshipped in different places and at different periods that the subject is a very confusing one, and is indeed the most difficult problem in Egyptology.

RÄ was the great god of the Egyptians, and regarded by them as the great Creator, is pictured as the sun, the life-giver; the other gods and goddesses were generally embodiments of his various attributes, or the eternal laws of nature; while some, like Osiris, were simply deified human beings. The different seats of the dynasties also had their various "triads," or trinities, of gods which they worshipped, while bulls and hawks, crocodiles and cats, have each in turn been venerated as emblems of some godlike or natural function. Thus the "scarab," or beetle, is the emblem of eternal life, for the Egyptians believed in a future state where the souls of men existed in a state of happiness or woe, according as their lives had been good or evil. But, like the hieroglyphs, this also is a study for scholars, and the ordinary visitor is content to admire the decorative effect these inscriptions give to walls and columns otherwise bare of ornament.

I must not close this slight sketch of its monuments without referring to the colossal statues so common in Egypt.

Babylonia has its winged bulls and kings of heroic size, Burma its built effigies of Buddha, but no country but Egypt has ever produced such mighty images as the monolith statues of her kings which adorn her many temples, and have their greatest expression in the rock-hewn temple of Abou Simbel and the imposing colossi of Thebes. In the case of Abou Simbel, the huge figures of Rameses II. which form the front of his temple are hewn out of the solid rock, and are 66 feet in height, forming one of the most impressive sights in Egypt. Though 6 feet less in height, the colossi of Thebes are even more striking, each figure being carved out of a single block of stone weighing many hundreds of tons, and which were transported from a great distance to be placed upon their pedestals in the plain of Thebes.

Surely in the old days of Egypt great ideas possessed the minds of men, and apart from the vastness of their other monuments, had ever kings before or since such impressive resting-places as the royal tombs cut deep into the bowels of the Theban hills, or the stupendous pyramids of Ghizeh!

CHAPTER IX
THE PEOPLE

Beyond everything else Egypt is an agricultural country, and the "fellahīn," or "soil-cutters," as the word means, its dominant type, and in order to form any idea of their character or mode of life, we must leave the towns behind and wander through the farm-lands of the Delta.

Trains are few, and hotels do not exist, and anyone wishing to see the people as they are must travel on horseback, and be content with such accommodation as the villages afford. The roads are the canal-banks, or little paths which wind among the fields; but, as we have already seen, the country has many beauties, and the people are so genuine in their simple hospitality that the traveller has many compensations for the incidental hardships he may undergo.

What will perhaps first strike the traveller is the industry of the people. The luxuriant crops give evidence of their labour, and the fields are everywhere alive. From dawn to dark everyone is busily employed, from the youngest child who watches the tethered cattle or brings water from the well, to the old man so soon to find his last resting-place in the picturesque "gabana"[9] without the village. Seed-time and harvest go side by side in Egypt, and one may often witness every operation of the farm, from ploughing to threshing, going on simultaneously. The people seem contented as they work, for whereas formerly the fellahīn were cruelly oppressed by their rulers, to-day, under British guidance, they have become independent and prosperous, and secure in the enjoyment of the fruits of their labour.

Another impression which the visitor will receive is the curiously Biblical character of their life, which constantly suggests the Old Testament stories; the shepherds watching their flocks, ring-streaked and speckled; the cattle ploughing in the

9 Cemetery.

fields; the women grinding at the handmill, or grouped about the village well, all recall incidents in the lives of Isaac and Rebekah, and episodes of patriarchal times. Their salutations and modes of speech are also Biblical, and lend a touch of poetry to their lives. "Turn in, my lord, turn in to me," was Jael's greeting to flying Sisera, and straight-way she prepared for him "butter in a lordly dish." So to-day hospitality is one of their cardinal virtues, and I have myself been chased by a horseman who rebuked me for having passed his home without refreshment.

Steam-pumps, cotton-mills, and railways may have slightly altered the aspect of the country, but to all intents and purposes, in habit of thought and speech, in costume and customs, the people remain to-day much as they were in those remote times pictured in the Book of Genesis.

Fresh fruit or coffee is frequently proffered to the traveller on his way, while his welcome at a village or the house of some landed proprietor is always sure. On approaching a village, which is often surrounded by dense groves of date-palms, the traveller will be met by the head men, who, with many salaams, conduct him to the village "mandareh," or rest-house, and it is only as such a guest, resident in a village, that one can form any idea of the home-life of the people.

From the outside the village often has the appearance of some rude fortification, the houses practically joining each other and their mud-walls having few openings. Within, narrow and tortuous lanes form the only thoroughfares, which terminate in massive wooden doors, which are closed at night and guarded by the village watchman. The huts--for they are nothing else--which compose the village are seldom of more than one storey, while in many cases their small doorway forms their only means of ventilation. Their roofs are covered with a pile of cotton-stalks and other litter, through which the pungent smoke of their dung fires slowly percolates, while fowls and goats, and the inevitable pariah dog roam about them at will.

Windows, when they do occur, are merely slits in the mud wall, without glass or shutter, but often ornamented by a lattice of split palm-leaves. Light and ventilation practically do not exist, while a few mats, water-pots, and cooking utensils comprise the only furniture; yet the people are well-conditioned and content, for their life is in the fields, and their poor dwellings are little used except at meal-times or at night.

The guest-house is little better than the huts, except that one side is entirely open to the air; here at least the visitor may **breathe**, even though his slumbers may be disturbed by the sheep and cattle which wander in the lanes. At night a fire of corn-cobs is lit, and while its smoke serves to drive away the swarms of mosquitoes and flies with which the village is usually infested, its warmth is grateful, for the nights are cold, and by its light, aided by a few dim lanterns, the simple evening meal is shared with the head men, who count it an honour to entertain a guest.

I have described one of the poorest of the "fellah" villages, but the traveller is often more luxuriously housed. Many of the native landowners occupy roomy and well-appointed dwellings, often surrounded by pretty and well-stocked gardens, where one may rest beneath the vines and fig-trees, and enjoy the pomegranates, apricots, and other fruits which it supplies. These houses are generally clean and comfortably furnished after the Turkish manner. The host, prosperous-looking and well clothed, meets his guest at the doorstep or assists him to dismount, when, with many compliments and expressions of delight at his visit, he is conducted to the guest-chamber. Coffee and sweet meats are then presented, a foretaste of the generous meal to follow, for in the homes of the well-to-do a feast is usually provided for an honoured guest.

The food is served on the low "sahniyeh," or tray, which forms the table, on which several flat loaves surrounded by little dishes of salad and other condiments, mark the places of the diners; but before eating, each person present ceremoniously washes his hands and mouth, a servant bringing in the copper "tisht wa abrīk," or jug and basin, kept for that purpose.

The meal always begins with soup, which, greasy to begin with, is rendered more so by the addition of a bowl of melted butter. This is eaten with a spoon, the only utensil provided, each person dipping into the bowl, which is placed in the centre of the table. The rest of the meal, which consists of fish, pigeons, and various kinds of stews and salads, is eaten with the hands, the diners often presenting each other with choice morsels from their portion; a baked turkey stuffed with nuts, or on important occasions a whole sheep, forms the principal dish, which is cleverly divided by the host or principal guest without the aid of knife or fork. Water in porous jars, often flavoured with rose-leaves or verbena, is presented by servants as the meal proceeds. The final dish always consists of boiled rice and milk sweetened with honey, a delicious dish, which is eaten with the same spoon by which the soup was partaken of.

Such fare as I have described is only for the wealthy. In general the "fellahīn" live on rice and wheaten bread, sugar-cane, and vegetables, with the occasional addition of a little meat, or such fish as may be caught in the canals. Their beverage is water, coffee being a luxury only occasionally indulged in, and their use of tobacco is infrequent.

Theirs is a simple life whose daily round of labour is only broken by the occasional marriage feast, or village fair, or, in the more populous centres, by the periodic "MŪled," or religious festival.

In Cairo and other large cities, these "MŪleds" are very elaborate, and often last for days together. Then business is suspended, and, as at our Christmas-time, everyone gives himself up to enjoyment and the effort to make others happy. Gay booths are erected in the open spaces, in which is singing and the performance of strange Eastern dances. Mummers and conjurers perform in the streets, and merry-go-rounds and swing-boats amuse the youngsters, whose pleasure is further enhanced by the many stalls and barrows displaying toy balloons, dolls, and sweetmeats.

All wear their gayest clothing, and at night illuminations delight the hearts of these simple people.

The principal feasts are the "MŪled-en-Nebbi," or birth of Mohammed, and "El HussanÊn," in memory of the martyred grandson of the Prophet, and although they are Mohammedans the "Eed-el-Imam," or birth of Christ, takes a high place among their religious celebrations.

But they have their fasts also, and Ramadan, which lasts for four weeks, is far more strictly observed than Lent among ourselves, for throughout that period, from sunrise to sunset, the Moslem abstains from food or drink, except in the case of the aged or infirm, or of anyone engaged upon work so arduous as to render food necessary, for the Mohammedan does not allow his religion to interfere with his other duties in life.

On the last day of Ramadan occurs a pretty observance similar to that of All Souls' day in France; then everyone visits the tombs of their relatives, laying garlands upon the graves and often passing the night in the cemeteries in little booths made for the purpose.

You will have noticed how large a place *religion* takes in the life of the people, and in their idle hours no subject of conversation is more common. To the average Mohammedan his religion is a very real matter in which he fervently believes, and Allah is to him a very personal God, whom he may at all times approach in praise or prayer in the certain belief of His fatherly care. Nothing impresses a traveller more than this tremendous belief of the Mohammedans in their Deity and their religion; and though many people, probably from lack of knowledge, hold the view that the Moslem faith is a debased one, it is in reality a fine religion, teaching many wise and beautiful doctrines, and ennobling the lives of all who live up to the best that is in it.

Unfortunately the teaching of Mohammedanism is so largely fatalistic that it tends to deprive the individual of personal initiative. "The Lord gave, and the Lord hath taken away, blessed be the name of the Lord," is a general attitude of mind, and this, combined with their long centuries of servitude, has had so much effect upon the national character of the Egyptian that they almost entirely lack those qualities of alertness, confidence, and sense of personal responsibility without which no race can become great or even, indeed, be self-respecting.

The higher education now general in Egypt has already had its effect upon the present generation, among which a feeling of ambition and independence is grow-ing, while the Egyptian army has shown what wonders may be wrought, even with the poorest material, by sustained and honest effort in the right direction; and if the just and sympathetic guidance which it has enjoyed for now a quarter of a century is not too soon withdrawn, Egypt may once again become a nation.

As it is, to-day the great mass of the people remain much as they have been for ages; a simple, kindly people, ignorant and often fanatical, but broadly good-humoured and keenly alive to a joke; fond of their children, and showing great consideration for age, they have many traits which endear them to those who have lived among them, while their faults are largely on the surface, and due in some measure to the centuries of ignorance and slavery which has been their lot.

The greatest blot upon the Egyptian character is the position accorded to their women, who, as in all Mohammedan countries, are considered to be soulless. From infancy employed in the most menial occupations, they are not even permitted to enter the mosques at prayer-time, and until recently the scanty education which the boys enjoyed was denied to their sisters. It is no wonder, therefore, that these often beautiful girls grow up much like graceful animals, ignorant of the higher duties of life, and exercising none of that refining and ennobling influence which have made the Western races what they are.

CHAPTER X
THE DESERT

When so much of geographical Egypt consists of desert, it would be interesting if I were to tell you something about it before closing this little book. Probably the first question my readers would ask would be, "What use is it?" Why does Nature create such vast wastes of land and rock which can be of little or no use to anybody?

We cannot always follow the intentions of Nature, or see what may ultimately result, but so far as the desert is concerned we know of at least *one* useful purpose it serves, and that is the making of *climate*.

Edinburgh and Moscow are in precisely the same latitudes, yet the one is equable in temperature while the other endures the rigours of an arctic winter. The South of Iceland also suffers less from cold than do the great central plains of Europe. And why? Simply because their different climates are the result of special conditions or influences of Nature, and what the Gulf Stream does for the British Isles the deserts of Africa effect not only for Egypt, but for the whole of Southern Europe, whose genial climate is mainly caused by the warm air generated on these sun-baked barren lands.

Now let us see what the desert is like in appearance. It is a very common impression that the desert is simply a flat expanse of sand, colourless and unbroken; in reality it is quite different, being full of variations, which give it much the same diversity of interest as the ocean.

The colour of the sand varies infinitely, according to its situation. Thus the desert which surrounds Assuan, which is composed of decimated granite and Nile silt, is generally grey; in Nubia the sand is formed of powdered sandstone of a curiously golden tint, while the desert of Suez, which abuts on Cairo and the Delta provinces, is generally white in tone, due to the admixture of limestone dust of which it is largely composed. The great Sahara also is no monotonous stretch of sand, but is to a great extent covered by wild herbs of many kinds, which often entirely screen the sand from view, and give it the appearance of a prairie.

Nor is the desert always flat, for its huge undulations suggest ocean billows petrified into stillness, while rocky hills and earthquake-riven valleys give it a fantastic variety which is wildly picturesque.

Though generally barren, the desert supports growths of many kinds; wild hyssop, thorns, the succulent ice-plant, and a great variety of other shrubs. Flowers also abound, and though they are usually small, I have counted as many as twenty varieties in an area of as many feet, and in some of the deep "wadis," as the mountain valleys are called, wild plants grow in such profusion as to give them the appearance of rock gardens.

In aspect the desert varies very much, according to the time of day or changing effect of light.

At dawn a curious mauve tint suffuses it, and the sun rises sharp and clear above the horizon, which also stands out crisply against the sky, so pure is the air. Presently, as the sun slowly rises higher in the sky, every shrub or stone or little inequality of surface is tipped with gold and throws long blue shadows across the sand. At midday a fierce glare envelops it, obliterating detail and colour, while by moonlight it is a fairyland of silver, solemn, still, and mysterious. Each phase has its special beauty, which interests the traveller and robs his journey of monotony.

Scattered over the surface of the sand are innumerable pebbles of all sizes and colours--onyx, cornelian, agate, and many more, as well as sea fossils and other petrifactions which boys would love to collect. And it is also curious to notice that the rocks which crop up in all directions become *sunburnt*, and limestone, naturally of a dazzling white, often assumes a variety of tints under the influence of the powerful sun, as may be seen in the foreground of my picture of the pyramids.

Animal life also exists in profusion; every tuft of scrub supports a variety of insects upon which the hunting spider and desert lizard feed; the tracks of giant beetles or timid jerboa scour the sand in all directions, and many wild-birds make these wastes their home. Prowling wolves and foxes hunt the tiny gazelle, while the rocky hills, in which the wild goats make their home, also give shelter to the hyenas and jackals, which haunt the caravan routes to feast upon the dying animals which fall abandoned to their fate.

The life of the desert is not confined to the beasts, however, for many Bedawīn tribes roam about them in search of water or fodder for their animals, and of all the Eastern races I have met none are more interesting than these desert nomads.

The wandering life of the Bedawīn makes it difficult for anyone to become acquainted with them, while their reputation for lawlessness is such that travellers on desert routes usually endeavour to avoid them. In several parts of the desert near Egypt, however, important families of them have settled so as to be near the farm-lands granted to them by Ismail Pasha many years ago (nominally in return for military services, but in reality to keep them quiet), and I have often visited their camps at Beni Ayoub and Tel Bedawi, to find them courteous, hospitable, and in the best sense of the word, gentlemen.

These camps are large, and the long lines of tents, pitched with military precision, shelter probably more than 1,000 people, for though the head sheykh may build a lodge of stone in which to entertain his guests, the Arab is a gipsy who loves his tent.

The tents, which are often very large, are formed of heavy cloths of goats'-hair woven in stripes of different colours, and supported by a large number of poles; long tassels hang from the seams, and other cloths are often attached to them so as to divide the tent into different apartments. Clean sand forms the floor, on which at nightfall a rug or carpet is spread to form a bed. Round the walls are the gay saddle-bags and trappings of the camels and horses, as well as many boxes ornamented with tinsel and painting, which contain the wardrobes and other possessions of the inmates. At the tent-door, stuck upright in the ground, is the long spear of its occupant, and the large earthen pot which serves as fireplace, while in some shady corner a row of zīrs contain their supply of drinking water. Turkeys and fowl give a homely look to the premises, where perhaps a gentle-eyed gazelle is playmate to the rough-haired dogs few Bedawīn are without. Round about the tents children are playing, while their mothers are working at the hand-loom, or preparing the simple evening meal.

In character the Bedawīn are dignified and reserved, and have a great contempt for the noisiness so characteristic of the Egyptians, but, like them, are passionately fond of their wives and children, and so highly prize the various articles of saddlery or apparel made by their hands that no money would buy them.

The men are tall, with strong aquiline features and keen eyes, which look very piercing beneath the "cufia,"[10] which is wrapped around their heads; their clothing is loose and flowing, a black "arbiyeh" being worn over the "khaftan," or inner robe, of white or coloured stripes, and their boots are of soft leather. Though the traditional spear is still retained, all are armed with some firearm--ancient flint-locks of great length, or more commonly nowadays with a modern rifle, and many of the sheykhs wear a long, curved sword of beautiful workmanship, which is slung across their shoulders by a silken cord. All have strong, deep voices, and impress you with the idea that these are manly and courageous fellows, and upright according to their lights.

The women also are clothed in loose draperies, the outer one of some rough material, which conceals others of daintier fabric and colour. Handsome in feature, with glossy blue-black hair, their dark gipsy faces also wear that look of sturdy independence which so becomes the men.

It may naturally be asked, "How do these people occupy their time?" First of all, they have large flocks, which must be fed and watered, and they are thus compelled to wander from well to well, or from one oasis to another, and they are also great breeders of horses, which must be carefully looked after, and from time to time taken to some far away fair for sale. Food and water also have often to be brought long distances to their camps by the camel-men, while the women are occupied with their domestic duties and their weaving.

Naturally the Bedawīn are expert horsemen, and are very fond of equestrian sports. Some of their fancy riding is very clever, and great rivalry exists among them, particularly in their "jerīd," or javelin, play, when frequently several hundreds of mounted men are engaged in a mÊlÃ©e, which, though only intended to be a friendly contest, often results in serious injury or death to many.

The Arab is very fond of his horse, which he himself has bred and trained from a colt, and his affection is amply returned by his steed. They are beautiful animals, strong and fleet-footed, but often savage with anyone but their master.

Sport enters largely into the life of the Bedawīn, and many tribes train falcons,

---

10   A square shawl of white or coloured silk.

with which they hunt gazelles, and in the Lybian desert the "cheetah," or hunting leopard, is tamed and used for the same purpose, and in this way the monotony of many a long desert march is relieved.

When on a journey smaller tents than those which I have described are used, all the heavy baggage being loaded on to camels, upon which the women and children also ride. Camels have often been called the "ships of the desert," and they are certainly the most useful of all animals for such travelling, for their broad pads prevent their feet from sinking into the soft sand, and not only do they carry enormous loads, but are able for days together to go without food or water. When Abraham sent his servant to seek a wife for Isaac, it was on camels that he travelled, and shaded, no doubt, by her canopy of shawls, it was on camel-back that Rebekah returned with him to the tent of his master. So to-day we may often meet a similar party on their journey, the women seated beneath the "mahmal," as the canopy is called, while the food and water for the journey is slung from the saddles of the camels ridden by the armed men who form their escort.

Camels are of two kinds--the heavily-built beast, such as we see in Egypt, and which is used for baggage purposes, and the "hagīn," or dromedary, used solely for riding. Lest any of my readers should fall into the common error of supposing that the dromedary has two humps, let me say that the only difference between it and the ordinary camel is that it is smaller and better bred, just as our racehorses differ from draught animals, and must not be confounded with the Bactrian or two-humped camel of Asia. These hagīn are very fleet, and often cover great distances, and I have known one to travel as much as 100 miles between sunset and sunrise!

On a journey the pace of a caravan is that of its slowest beast, and very arduous such journeys often are, for there is no shade, and the dust raised by the caravan envelops the slowly moving travellers, while the fierce sun is reflected from the rocks, which often become too hot to touch. On the other hand, the nights are often bitterly cold, for the sand is too loose to retain any of its heat, while the salt with which the desert is strongly impregnated has a chilling effect on the air. Most trying of all, however, are the hot desert winds, which often last for days together, drying up the water in the skins, while the distressed travellers are half suffocated by the dust and flying sand which cut the skin like knives. Little wonder, therefore, if these hardy desert tribes are taciturn and reserved, for they see nature in its stern moods, and know little of that ease of life which may be experienced among the green crops and pastures of the Delta.

It must not be supposed that the Bedawīn are morose, for beneath their outward severity lies a great power for sympathy and affection. The love of the Arab for his horse is proverbial, and his kindness to all dumb animals is remarkable.

Like the Egyptian, family affection holds him strongly, and he has a keen appreciation of poetry and music. Hospitality is to him a law, and the guest is always treated with honour; it is pleasant also to see the respect with which the Bedawīn regard their women, and the harmony which exists between the members or a tribe. Their government is patriarchal, each tribe being ruled by its sheykh, the "father of his children," who administers their code of honour or justice, and whose decision is always implicitly obeyed. Here, again, we have another Biblical parallel, for, like his brother Mohammedan in Egypt, the life of the desert Arab, no less than the dwellers on the "black soil," still preserves many of those poetical customs and characteristics which render the history of Abraham so attractive, and although these pages have only been able to give a partial picture of Egypt and its people, perhaps enough has been said to induce my readers to learn more about them, as well as to enable them a little more fully to realize how very real, and how very human, are the romantic stories of the Old Testament.

The Codes Of Hammurabi And Moses
W. W. Davies

QTY

The discovery of the Hammurabi Code is one of the greatest achievements of archaeology, and is of paramount interest, not only to the student of the Bible, but also to all those interested in ancient history...

Religion   ISBN: *1-59462-338-4*   Pages:132

MSRP $12.95

The Theory of Moral Sentiments
Adam Smith

QTY

This work from 1749. contains original theories of conscience amd moral judgment and it is the foundation for systemof morals.

Philosophy ISBN: *1-59462-777-0*   Pages:536

MSRP $19.95

Jessica's First Prayer
Hesba Stretton

QTY

In a screened and secluded corner of one of the many railway-bridges which span the streets of London there could be seen a few years ago, from five o'clock every morning until half past eight, a tidily set-out coffee-stall, consisting of a trestle and board, upon which stood two large tin cans, with a small fire of charcoal burning under each so as to keep the coffee boiling during the early hours of the morning when the work-people were thronging into the city on their way to their daily toil...

Childrens   ISBN: *1-59462-373-2*

Pages:84

MSRP $9.95

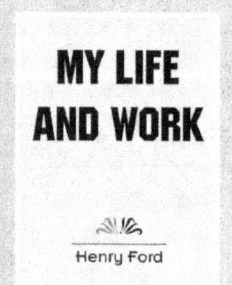

My Life and Work
Henry Ford

QTY

Henry Ford revolutionized the world with his implementation of mass production for the Model T automobile. Gain valuable business insight into his life and work with his own auto-biography... "We have only started on our development of our country we have not as yet, with all our talk of wonderful progress, done more than scratch the surface. The progress has been wonderful enough but..."

Biographies/   ISBN: *1-59462-198-5*

Pages:300

MSRP $21.95

The Art of Cross-Examination
Francis Wellman

QTY

I presume it is the experience of every author, after his first book is published upon an important subject, to be almost overwhelmed with a wealth of ideas and illustrations which could readily have been included in his book, and which to his own mind, at least, seem to make a second edition inevitable. Such certainly was the case with me; and when the first edition had reached its sixth impression in five months, I rejoiced to learn that it seemed to my publishers that the book had met with a sufficiently favorable reception to justify a second and considerably enlarged edition. ..

Pages:412

Reference   **ISBN:** *1-59462-647-2*   *MSRP $19.95*

On the Duty of Civil Disobedience
Henry David Thoreau

QTY

Thoreau wrote his famous essay, On the Duty of Civil Disobedience, as a protest against an unjust but popular war and the immoral but popular institution of slave-owning. He did more than write—he declined to pay his taxes, and was hauled off to gaol in consequence. Who can say how much this refusal of his hastened the end of the war and of slavery ?

Law   **ISBN:** *1-59462-747-9*   **Pages:48**

MSRP $7.45

Dream Psychology Psychoanalysis for Beginners
Sigmund Freud

QTY

Sigmund Freud, born Sigismund Schlomo Freud (May 6, 1856 - September 23, 1939), was a Jewish-Austrian neurologist and psychiatrist who co-founded the psychoanalytic school of psychology. Freud is best known for his theories of the unconscious mind, especially involving the mechanism of repression; his redefinition of sexual desire as mobile and directed towards a wide variety of objects; and his therapeutic techniques, especially his understanding of transference in the therapeutic relationship and the presumed value of dreams as sources of insight into unconscious desires.

Pages:196

Psychology   **ISBN:** *1-59462-905-6*   *MSRP $15.45*

The Miracle of Right Thought
Orison Swett Marden

QTY

Believe with all of your heart that you will do what you were made to do. When the mind has once formed the habit of holding cheerful, happy, prosperous pictures, it will not be easy to form the opposite habit. It does not matter how improbable or how far away this realization may see, or how dark the prospects may be, if we visualize them as best we can, as vividly as possible, hold tenaciously to them and vigorously struggle to attain them, they will gradually become actualized, realized in the life. But a desire, a longing without endeavor, a yearning abandoned or held indifferently will vanish without realization.

Pages:360

Self Help   **ISBN:** *1-59462-644-8*   *MSRP $25.45*

QTY

The Rosicrucian Cosmo-Conception Mystic Christianity by *Max Heindel*   ISBN: *1-59462-188-8*   **$38.95**
The Rosicrucian Cosmo-conception is not dogmatic, neither does it appeal to any other authority than the reason of the student. It is: not controversial, but is: sent forth in the, hope that it may help to clear...   New Age/Religion Pages 646

Abandonment To Divine Providence by *Jean-Pierre de Caussade*   ISBN: *1-59462-228-0*   **$25.95**
"The Rev. Jean Pierre de Caussade was one of the most remarkable spiritual writers of the Society of Jesus in France in the 18th Century. His death took place at Toulouse in 1751. His works have gone through many editions and have been republished...   Inspirational/Religion Pages 400

Mental Chemistry by *Charles Haanel*   ISBN: *1-59462-192-6*   **$23.95**
Mental Chemistry allows the change of material conditions by combining and appropriately utilizing the power of the mind. Much like applied chemistry creates something new and unique out of careful combinations of chemicals the mastery of mental chemistry...   New Age Pages 354

The Letters of Robert Browning and Elizabeth Barret Barrett 1845-1846 vol II   ISBN: *1-59462-193-4*   **$35.95**
by *Robert Browning* and *Elizabeth Barrett*   Biographies Pages 596

Gleanings In Genesis (volume I) by *Arthur W. Pink*   ISBN: *1-59462-130-6*   **$27.45**
Appropriately has Genesis been termed "the seed plot of the Bible" for in it we have, in germ form, almost all of the great doctrines which are afterwards fully developed in the books of Scripture which follow...   Religion/Inspirational Pages 420

The Master Key by *L. W. de Laurence*   ISBN: *1-59462-001-6*   **$30.95**
In no branch of human knowledge has there been a more lively increase of the spirit of research during the past few years than in the study of Psychology, Concentration and Mental Discipline. The requests for authentic lessons in Thought Control, Mental Discipline and...   New Age/Business Pages 422

The Lesser Key Of Solomon Goetia by *L. W. de Laurence*   ISBN: *1-59462-092-X*   **$9.95**
This translation of the first book of the "Lemegeton" which is now for the first time made accessible to students of Talismanic Magic was done, after careful collation and edition, from numerous Ancient Manuscripts in Hebrew, Latin, and French...   New Age/Occult Pages 92

Rubaiyat Of Omar Khayyam by *Edward Fitzgerald*   ISBN: *1-59462-332-5*   **$13.95**
Edward Fitzgerald, whom the world has already learned, in spite of his own efforts to remain within the shadow of anonymity, to look upon as one of the rarest poets of the century, was born at Bredfield, in Suffolk, on the 31st of March, 1809. He was the third son of John Purcell...   Music Pages 172

Ancient Law by *Henry Maine*   ISBN: *1-59462-128-4*   **$29.95**
The chief object of the following pages is to indicate some of the earliest ideas of mankind, as they are reflected in Ancient Law, and to point out the relation of those ideas to modern thought.   Religion/History Pages 452

Far-Away Stories by *William J. Locke*   ISBN: *1-59462-129-2*   **$19.45**
"Good wine needs no bush, but a collection of mixed vintages does. And this book is just such a collection. Some of the stories I do not want to remain buried for ever in the museum files of dead magazine-numbers an author's not unpardonable vanity..."   Fiction Pages 272

Life of David Crockett by *David Crockett*   ISBN: *1-59462-250-7*   **$27.45**
"Colonel David Crockett was one of the most remarkable men of the times in which he lived. Born in humble life, but gifted with a strong will, an indomitable courage, and unremitting perseverance...   Biographies/New Age Pages 424

Lip-Reading by *Edward Nitchie*   ISBN: *1-59462-206-X*   **$25.95**
Edward B. Nitchie, founder of the New York School for the Hard of Hearing, now the Nitchie School of Lip-Reading, Inc, wrote "LIP-READING Principles and Practice". The development and perfecting of this meritorious work on lip-reading was an undertaking...   How-to Pages 400

A Handbook of Suggestive Therapeutics, Applied Hypnotism, Psychic Science   ISBN: *1-59462-214-0*   **$24.95**
by *Henry Munro*   Health/New Age/Health/Self-help Pages 376

A Doll's House: and Two Other Plays by *Henrik Ibsen*   ISBN: *1-59462-112-8*   **$19.95**
Henrik Ibsen created this classic when in revolutionary 1848 Rome. Introducing some striking concepts in playwriting for the realist genre, this play has been studied the world over.   Fiction/Classics/Plays 308

The Light of Asia by *sir Edwin Arnold*   ISBN: *1-59462-204-3*   **$13.95**
In this poetic masterpiece, Edwin Arnold describes the life and teachings of Buddha. The man who was to become known as Buddha to the world was born as Prince Gautama of India but he rejected the worldly riches and abandoned the reigns of power when...   Religion/History/Biographies Pages 170

The Complete Works of Guy de Maupassant by *Guy de Maupassant*   ISBN: *1-59462-157-8*   **$16.95**
"For days and days, nights and nights, I had dreamed of that first kiss which was to consecrate our engagement, and I knew not on what spot I should put my lips..."   Fiction/Classics Pages 240

The Art of Cross-Examination by *Francis L. Wellman*   ISBN: *1-59462-309-0*   **$26.95**
Written by a renowned trial lawyer, Wellman imparts his experience and uses case studies to explain how to use psychology to extract desired information through questioning.   How-to/Science/Reference Pages 408

Answered or Unanswered? by *Louisa Vaughan*   ISBN: *1-59462-248-5*   **$10.95**
Miracles of Faith in China   Religion Pages 112

The Edinburgh Lectures on Mental Science (1909) by *Thomas*   ISBN: *1-59462-008-3*   **$11.95**
This book contains the substance of a course of lectures recently given by the writer in the Queen Street Hall, Edinburgh. Its purpose is to indicate the Natural Principles governing the relation between Mental Action and Material Conditions...   New Age/Psychology Pages 148

Ayesha by *H. Rider Haggard*   ISBN: *1-59462-301-5*   **$24.95**
Verily and indeed it is the unexpected that happens! Probably if there was one person upon the earth from whom the Editor of this, and of a certain previous history, did not expect to hear again...   Classics Pages 380

Ayala's Angel by *Anthony Trollope*   ISBN: *1-59462-352-X*   **$29.95**
The two girls were both pretty, but Lucy who was twenty-one who supposed to be simple and comparatively unattractive, whereas Ayala was credited, as her Bombwhat romantic name might show, with poetic charm and a taste for romance. Ayala when her father died was nineteen...   Fiction Pages 484

The American Commonwealth by *James Bryce*   ISBN: *1-59462-286-8*   **$34.45**
An interpretation of American democratic political theory. It examines political mechanics and society from the perspective of Scotsman James Bryce   Politics Pages 572

Stories of the Pilgrims by *Margaret P. Pumphrey*   ISBN: *1-59462-116-0*   **$17.95**
This book explores pilgrims religious oppression in England as well as their escape to Holland and eventual crossing to America on the Mayflower, and their early days in New England...   History Pages 268

QTY

The Fasting Cure *by Sinclair Upton*   ISBN: *1-59462-222-1* **$13.95**

In the Cosmopolitan Magazine for May, 1910, and in the Contemporary Review (London) for April, 1910, I published an article dealing with my experiences in fasting. I have written a great many magazine articles, but never one which attracted so much attention... New Age/Self Help/Health Pages 164

Hebrew Astrology *by Sepharial*   ISBN: *1-59462-308-2* **$13.45**

In these days of advanced thinking it is a matter of common observation that we have left many of the old landmarks behind and that we are now pressing forward to greater heights and to a wider horizon than that which represented the mind-content of our progenitors... Astrology Pages 144

Thought Vibration or The Law of Attraction in the Thought World   ISBN: *1-59462-127-6* **$12.95**

by William Walker Atkinson   Psychology/Religion Pages 144

Optimism *by Helen Keller*   ISBN: *1-59462-108-X* **$15.95**

Helen Keller was blind, deaf, and mute since 19 months old, yet famously learned how to overcome these handicaps, communicate with the world, and spread her lectures promoting optimism. An inspiring read for everyone... Biographies/Inspirational Pages 84

Sara Crewe *by Frances Burnett*   ISBN: *1-59462-360-0* **$9.45**

In the first place, Miss Minchin lived in London. Her home was a large, dull, tall one, in a large, dull square, where all the houses were alike, and all the sparrows were alike, and where all the door-knockers made the same heavy sound... Childrens/Classic Pages 88

The Autobiography of Benjamin Franklin *by Benjamin Franklin*   ISBN: *1-59462-135-7* **$24.95**

The Autobiography of Benjamin Franklin has probably been more extensively read than any other American historical work, and no other book of its kind has had such ups and downs of fortune. Franklin lived for many years in England, where he was agent... Biographies/History Pages 332

Name	
Email	
Telephone	
Address	
City, State ZIP	

☐ **Credit Card**   ☐ **Check / Money Order**

Credit Card Number	
Expiration Date	
Signature	

Please Mail to: Book Jungle
                  PO Box 2226
                  Champaign, IL 61825
or Fax to: 630-214-0564

ORDERING INFORMATION

web: *www.bookjungle.com*
email: *sales@bookjungle.com*
fax: *630-214-0564*
mail: *Book Jungle PO Box 2226 Champaign, IL 61825*
or PayPal *to sales@bookjungle.com*

Please contact us for bulk discounts

DIRECT-ORDER TERMS

**20% Discount if You Order
Two or More Books**
Free Domestic Shipping!
Accepted: Master Card, Visa,
Discover, American Express

www.ingramcontent.com/pod-product-compliance
Lightning Source LLC
Chambersburg PA
CBHW081305200626
46813CB00018B/3261